A CRY OF BEES

MELISSA HARDY

A Cry of Bees

NEW YORK / THE VIKING PRESS

813.54
H 2 2 c
73089
January, 1971

First published in 1970 by The Viking Press, Inc.
625 Madison Avenue, New York, N.Y. 10022

Published simultaneously in Canada by
The Macmillan Company of Canada Limited

SBN 670-25048-1
Library of Congress catalog card number: 78-104133

Printed in U.S.A. by Vail-Ballou Press, Inc.

FOR MY FATHER

A CRY OF BEES

CHAPTER *One*

There was a stillness when the air breathed heavy with the promise of snow. Silence swallowed the town, and in its belly all lay thick and quiet and ripe. The clouds that constituted the winter sky hovered a moment before blossoming in snow. Their moment was, to us, days. We were all caught in it, in the waiting.

Mrs. Logg sat in the living room of my Uncle Lamb's boarding house, and with one hand pried the rolled top of her nylon away from the abundant flesh of her knee, leaving a thick pink line in the rubber-textured flesh. She scratched at it with long, jagged fingernails.

"Bosoms, Emmeline," said Miss Rama Stalk, aiming at my ear, "are exorbitant pieces of fatty flesh, and unsightly in most cases due to a lack of support." She thumped her own bony chest, which boasted three round lumps of flesh, hard, like small, stale breads set in a row for the crows to eat. Two were breasts. The other was a tumor. "That is why I am proud to be almost completely flat-chested."

Mrs. Logg, insensible to criticism of so large a portion of her anatomy, sat sprawled in the green wicker chair, her bosom in an advanced stage of abandonment and, at this hour of the day, almost completely unfurled.

"I wear a bust confiner myself," said Miss Tibbitt.

There came a dry munching from inside the covered birdcage wherein she kept her pet rabbit, Glorio.

"Is that rabbit eating himself again?"

She picked up the cover. There sat Glorio, chewing on a hind leg.

"Glorio!" exclaimed Miss Tibbitt. "Stop that dreadful chewing!"

Glorio had this thing. He ate himself. No cunning bunny, Glorio was in every way fearless, in every way but one. And that one was lightning.

Glorio was terrified of lightning.

Perhaps lightning awakened in Glorio some long-hidden instinct, a deep and dark and treacherous memory that dwelt, an unnamed thing, in his little black brain.

Whatever Glorio's secret was, lightning held him firm in its grasp. It was his master, his torment, his god—it mesmerized him. His eyes, once cold and icebound balls sliding slowly from one end of their narrow sockets to the other, became transfixed. They spread in his face. They grew and they grew until they swelled and became the size of marbles, until the pinpoints of red had swallowed all the pupil, replacing the eye of a clever and evil rabbit with those of a rabbit bewitched.

Upon the advent of a thunderstorm Glorio had once been wont to charge over to the corner where Miss Tibbitt kept his lettuce and there to chomp up everything in sight.

One night, however, during an especially long and sky-brightening series of nature's fireworks, Glorio hit rock bottom—to be more precise, rock carpet.

There being no other alternative, and the vegetarian Glorio having long yearned for a taste of flesh, he lost no time in applying himself to the meat at hand, that in the nearest proximity being himself. From that moment on, Glorio was a meat man. His lettuce languished in its corner.

As a result of this unrabbitly food pattern, Glorio roamed the world decked out in a singularly revolting set of scabs.

At the merest suggestion of thunder on the horizon, when he smelled that special, tense, vibrant odor of a storm in the making—an odor blowing in on the warm and water-heavy breeze that sprang up off the river, traveling lackadaisically through the town, stopping, sitting down to iced coffee or ginger water, wafting its way finally to the pink and storm-searching nose of Glorio—he would dispatch himself to his corner and commence chomping himself with unbelievable enthusiasm.

This continued for about a month.

Then Glorio, deciding that, being a rabbit, his days were numbered on this earth, that Sunday was every day, that life is for the living, that life itself is a storm, took to digesting himself just any old time.

"Glorio!" Miss Tibbitt swatted the cage with a doily. "Glorio! You'll *bleed!*"

Miss Rama looked up in horror.

Glorio gave her the eye and spat out his foot.

Miss Tibbitt lowered the cage cover.

"Nasty chewing," she muttered. "He just bleeds all over everything."

Lucinda, our maid, moved her tremendous bulk through the dining room, seized a doily from the top of the chair nearest the moosehead, and scurried off into the kitchen.

I heard a dim scuffling from back of the kitchen porch.

I stood up from the floor where I had been sitting, stuffed my underwear, which was in reality Miss Tibbitt's, down into my overalls, and walked into the dining room.

Mrs. Turncew had Uncle by one hand and was trying to pull him off the chicken coop.

I watched them through the window. I wiped my nose on a large hunk of underwear I brought out of the vast collection of folds and elastics Miss Tibbitt's immense drawers provided me with. I went back and sat on the floor of the foyer.

"Unavieve Macc can't figure out when Passover is," said Mrs. Logg, "so she's just gone ahead and put a big red X on her door anyway, and whenever anybody tries to get in, she just opens her upstairs window and yells, 'We are of Abraham. Angel of Death, pass us over!' and shuts it."

"She's a disgrace to the Methodist Church," said Rama Stalk.

While waiting for snow, I had flushed Mrs. Logg's rhinestone belt buckle down the commode in a fit of pique. Mrs. Logg, passing fond of the belt buckle, it having been given her by a long-ago lover, told me that the time had come to relinquish childish things—referring to the practice of flushing keepsakes from long-ago lovers down the commode—and become a man.

To my way of thinking, this seemed a completely unreasonable request. In the first place I was a girl. In the second, the belt buckle had returned the next morning, just a little worse for its underwater adventure, having been a trifle too large to trespass the portals of the Chaucy sewer system. And it was infinitely more valuable to her for this, its declaration of loyalty to its owner.

Deeply rooted in me, however, there was a fear of God, represented on earth by Mrs. Logg. My conscience informed me that this woman, who by her way of thinking had been so grossly wronged by me, was not long for this world—she being eighty-one, and cancerous when the spirit moved her—therefore it would not give me rest until such time as I had disposed of *some* childish thing.

I considered my Shirley Temple doll, who was bald. But fond memories of her more cunning moments drove me to rule out such a barbaric deed as doing away with her.

My jacks were infinitely precious to me.

My hoop was indispensable.

I searched my child's mind for some object childish but at the same time unlovable.

I thought of my marbles.

My marbles, of which there were two hundred and forty-eight, had been given me by a subsequently spurned love.

I had never seen the purpose of marbles.

They were round.

They were glass.

The opaque shooter could have fitted into my eye socket, had there not already been an eye occupying that position.

But the true *reason* for marbles escaped me.

I resolved that fate had decreed the marbles to perish, a scapegoat for all the various childish things I was too childish to put aside.

I thought on a fitting death.

I chose the furnace.

Outside there came a slight whistling of the wind as it snaked its way up from the river, where, in huge wedges of gray and muddy ice, the water lay, giving birth to breezes.

I could hear Uncle as he stood up on top of the chicken coop, arguing with Mrs. Turncew. "I will *not* come down! I like it up here!"

The sound of something metallic falling.

"*Go away!*"

Our furnace was a bastard thing. It crouched in the darkest corner of our cellar, a collector of cobwebs and, after the belt-buckle overboard incident, of marbles, thousands and thousands of marbles that I, in my winter tedium, my winter guilt, showered its open-holed radiators with.

Marbles are immortal. The marbles that I poured down the vents still linger in its grimy bowels, seethe, and occasionally rattle the ghost of their remains as hot air begins its long and unsuccessful climb to the heights, to the first floor, upon rare occasions to my room, to issue forth in black smoke, accompanied by ear-splitting screams and blasphemies, finally giving up and sliding back down the pipes to its mother fire.

A falling beer can from Uncle's hand cut the winter with its fall. In front of our house the hollow sound of steps clattered on the icy pavement.

Mrs. Logg rolled her bean-shaped black eyes toward the

window. "Don't look now, girls," she said, "but there goes Marble Freshower, that piece of pure flagrancy, and she's walking down the street in NAKED daylight!"

Miss Rama and Miss Tibbitt thumped their chests vehemently and wheezed.

Miss Kitty lay in her plump, acid-smelling chair. Her jawbone, as if it were unbending, slowly swung open—Miss Kitty was asleep. She was tall for her century, almost five seven, narrow throughout. Her chicken-like neck was a pole around which heavy, many-layered veins ran in twisted patterns after the manner of vines. This neck gave way to a chin from which the liver-spotted flesh hung in two limp folds. Her nose was long and narrow, indented at the tip, and her eyes were milky with a cataract that was just beginning to seize the sight of it. Her skin, which was a brown color underlaid with yellow, spotted, was in reality a mass of tiny lines, each the width of an end of a small and well-sharpened pencil. From this skin sprung wispy hairs, almost blond in their whiteness, which lay gentle against the leather of her ages-old skin. It smelled of sweet violet and clung in patches to her skull, through which her pate showed startling pink when compared to the rest of her skin. Miss Kitty was ninety-four.

"Do you know what she lets her niece do?" asked Miss Tibbitt in a tone of awe. She hit her bony knees together in an effort to propel some heat to her body. "That child Clara stands out on the corner of Milk and Jean, mind you, with nary a stitch of clothing under those itty-bitty see-through things she wears, *and* whenever cars go by . . . she picks up her dress just as brazen as *could be!*"

The ladies reared back in astonishment and thumped their chests once again.

Mrs. Logg pulled at the bosom of her dress. She was crammed and wedged into the already-mighty proportions of her dress, which, in the manner of all her dresses, was royal-blue and of satin. It was rather thin satin, with a tendency to unravel. It was black beneath the armhole and for a large portion of the outlaying area, with the residue of sweat. Mrs. Logg wedged a finger underneath the straining fabric, and from the foyer I could see the bulging outline of it through her dress. Mrs. Logg's bosom seemed the only part of her that had any vitality whatsoever. It seemed as if, when released, it would spring to energetic life with tremendous force.

"*No!* It's not cold!"

Several more beer cans met with frozen ground, and the sound of my uncle's voice came echoing through the house from the challenged top of the chicken coop.

"But Lamb!"

The ladies leaned toward the window where Marble Freshower could be seen weaving drunkenly down Jean Street. The slow slipping of her galoshes caught on the wet sheet of frost that the previous night had deposited on Chaucy.

"Her own sister's child!" exclaimed Miss Tibbitt sorrowfully.

This gave birth to a lengthy discussion as to the immorality and ill effects occasioned by the exposition of four-year-old Clara Freshower's nether regions, bared and, as it were, flapping in the breeze.

"Gootchey goo," said Miss Tibbitt. She leaned over the cage.

"No! I do not want a sweater!"

Miss Tibbitt looked up all of a sudden. "He bit my fingernail off," she said. "Glorio bit my fingernail off. Yesterday. I was going to send it to *Tinsel Talk*. They pay you five dollars for one two inches long and not cracked. Mine was nearly two inches long. I've been guarding it for weeks now."

She lifted up the cover of the cage. "I hope you choke on it!" She lowered the cage cover.

Uncle Lamb came striding through the living room, his great belly thrust out before him, his chin drawn in in such a way that it overlapped several times to touch with itself.

"No," he said, wheeling about on his heel. "I do *not* want any asparagus! It's *too* SOFT!"

Mrs. Turncew came following at his heels. "But Lamb, dear, it's good for you!" In her old white hands, where the veins had swelled to large and tubular size and been frozen thus, she carried a plate of asparagus, which, in its soft and eel-like state, leered at my uncle, occasionally throwing up little hisses of steam.

Uncle eyed it. *"No!"* he cried. With quick and decisive steps he strode toward the bathroom door.

Mrs. Turncew followed. Her heels hit every time in his shadow.

Uncle reached the bathroom door. He stopped. He thrust his hand out before him. "Madame!" he said. "I am going to the bathroom." He unzipped his pants with a flourish, opened the door, and slammed it in Mrs. Turncew's face.

Mrs. Turncew turned around. A wave of puzzlement rolled across her face. This, however, lasted for only a minute. In the next moment she was tittering. "Well, after all," Mrs. Turncew said to the ladies, "he's just like a little boy in some ways."

From the commode came the sound of three hard, rapid-fire flushes.

The asparagus writhed and seethed on the dish.

The ladies sat like upright urns in the living room. The fans that seemed in use each second—in the summer to beat the atmosphere into some semblance of ventilation, in the winter to catch selfishly at the heat which the furnace so grudgingly vomited up, and to hold it a minute—lay folded in ancient laps. The cold, shrouding the room as sheets shroud unused furniture seeped in must, lay unharassed on the air.

Like sleepwalkers my fingers made their slow and ritual journey from marble bag to radiator.

Far away, some bird brushed the quivering trees with its flight, and out of the dullness the bridge crawled like a tangled, many-legged spider across the broad gray face of the river frozen with weather. The sun lay many worlds away.

CHAPTER *Two*

Sometimes a song will bring it back. I hear it sometimes when I drive through the towns with my window rolled down, with the square, tangible blocks of yellow preheated sunlight coming in great three-dimensional masses to meet my eyes. It is on the street, on the lips of an old man, a child as young as I when it happened, heard and sometimes not heard. But it is there. In me there swells the memory of it. And sometimes the presence of it. I feel it very suddenly.

I am not a sentimental person. I travel these towns each day of my life. They are hot or cold with the temper of the Midwestern sun and the slowly shifting clock of seasons. They are leaf-shaded and quiet in places; in others they are hot and smell of metal burning.

But the song, the tune, the memory is there. Everywhere I go. In the very contours of the land, in the sweep of the hills, in the stretch of plains. And I remember it: it was cold, it was February, it was winter.

Winter blew in on the breath of a norther off the top of the river up Kokomo way that year. It whipped the leaves that lay first sodden with the rains of autumn, then dry with the advancement of the season, into a frantic death dance in the middle of Jean Street. The dust of leaf bones shifted over Chaucy. In an amber frost it sheathed it. The town lay still and waited for snow's coming.

Winter was a silent season. Ears were too crushed behind

the furry gray-or-brown earmuffs that Amberson's sold on their one-dollar grab-it table, the air was too thick with a sheet of gelled cold, to hear the unhappy noises people and cars made as they waddled, indistinct figures in a clouded atmosphere, through the streets of Chaucy caught in opaque.

We had lost one of our ladies at the boarding house that year, the ancient Mrs. Pennial. Inside the house came the soundless noise that waxes slow over the floors of places left empty by death—one less old lady's dry cough catching on the air, one less old lady's scuffs scratching at the floor. Death had picked her off like a clay pigeon thrown high on a clear day —it was as neat as a pin.

Uncle Lamb said that it was fate. Mrs. Pennial, who was very old and crisp, fragile as an ash, had done her duty by the earth when, after thirty-two years of marriage, she had wiped the grave dust off her Lady Angela gloves and deposited the husband she had been whittling on, shaping to the coffin, deep in the damp bone of earth.

Death, Uncle Lamb said, had fastened his sights on her then. He had his sights on all of us, on me, on him. It was only a matter of time.

Uncle threw me an empty beer can. I deposited it in the dark window of the chicken coop. The morning had been bright, clear-eyed, with the moon still hanging transparent on the painful blue of sky. Now a chill cloud hid the sun; clouds like balls rolled in cotton covered the sky. Snow.

"It's best not to marry, Emmeline," he said. "Women draw the fire."

Uncle Lamb did not approve of marriage. He had tasted it once. When he was a young man, twenty-five, he had married Miss Emmeline Russell from a farm east of Wapsippinicon. But Miss Emmeline had one day hopped the Cincinnati Bound, changed to the Katey Special in Kansas City, and invested herself in an unnatural relationship with Laurey Delaine, Mrs. Sumie's brother, in the nook town of Dennison,

Texas. When she died, four years after I was born, they had to peel the diamond rings off her fingers, white from having seen too much of the insides of Texas parlors; she wore both Uncle Lamb and Laurey's fortunes on her hands, twelve rings in all. Uncle wouldn't take his six back. He sent one yellow rose instead.

I could see the logic behind not marrying. Mrs. Pennial had been married, and Mrs. Winslow, who had died the June before with a flourish of lilies and several clusters of grapes. And, God rest their souls, they were dead now, dead as nits, laid six feet under the other side of Beekerman's Hill.

The Lambs, being a comfort-loving people, had not taken kindly to spending all that portion of eternity remaining to them in a cold bed. "Fire next time," said my second cousin, Mrs. Sumie Delaine, and she proceeded to have herself cremated.

The remainder of my relations followed suit by all disposing of themselves in like manner, and as the years outlived each other the number of urns in which their ashes lay grew until the entire left and right corner catch-it-alls were abloom with vases and vessels of various shapes and sizes.

My Uncle Robbley's was the one I remember most distinctly. It was tall, nearly four feet tall, and so wide and round that I, as a child, could scarcely wrap my arms about it.

Various aunts who were, needless to say, not blood but ties hinted that Uncle Robbley's was a scandalous waste of urn, seeing as how there were so few ashes—it having been a windy day and Uncle Robbley a skinny man. So skinny, said my Aunt Tran, you could have threaded a candle with him if you'd taken a mind to do such a foolish thing, and practically twice as mean.

Uncle Lamb took the top off the urn and used it for his cigar ashes, the mingling of the two having augmented the amount by nearly four times its original content.

After this warning about marriage from Uncle Lamb, I betook myself to the living room to examine the name plates on the urns: Aunt Rene, my Grandfather Lamb, my famous cousin Mrs. Sumie Delaine—all in all, there were eleven urns, and only one resident of those eleven had not been married: Uncle Cobb, whose ashes, having been thrown away by accident, of course didn't count.

I walked around the dimmed parlor. Outside, the snow that kept Chaucy captive from November to the last days of March spread slow and glistened with ice as the river slowly swallowed the sun.

I turned and looked through the house, through the dining room where the shadows of bare branches cast their runes upon the scratched table and cut through the small gray kitchen; I looked through the window at my uncle, who sat in a straight-back chair on top of the chicken coop.

Snow, coming with the night, was just beginning to fall, slow and straight, like weights thrown from heaven. It fogged the lines of his silhouette. He became only a mass, indistinct in the twilight.

I thought momentarily on the great black benches that crouched at every bus stop—a gift to the citizenry of Chaucy from the Boxwright Brothers' Funeral Supply and Co-operative. They reached out with long arms and drew you to them. You slid into their depths with a feeling of awe and of fear.

The command COME TO US IN YOUR HOUR OF GRIEF breathed hot in letters of white on the back of your captive neck; caught as you were within the crouching black box of bench, you could see nothing, nothing but the two twin peaks of your knees rising hesitantly above you.

In the soft and silent safety of the snow, I thought how safe we were, he and I: me only eight, him a man, now unmarried. I forgot that there were ways of killing a man indirectly—with a sugar-sheathed bullet.

It was that winter that Mrs. Turncew, our neighbor to the corner of Marley and Lee Ambrose, finished her woman's task.

After having returned to earth her husband Arthur, all gray and rounded off at the edges, Mrs. Turncew brushed the grave dust off her Lady Angela gloves. She came after Uncle Lamb.

CHAPTER *Three*

"Oh Lamb," said Mrs. Turncew.

"What?" said Uncle Lamb. "Lucinda," he said, "put that ta-blecloth down—put it back where it belongs. It's the only one clean."

Lucinda was the old colored woman Mrs. Sumie Delaine had brought up from Dennison when she had come north to this river fork fifty years before. Lucinda was ancient and composed almost entirely of loose, yellow-gray folds of flesh, as if her color had been painted over fat gray ash. Her face, with its tiny features, its turned-up, unnegroid nose, bordered on the fragile. Her eyes, minute, were fixed deep into her bone, and her eyebrows were almost nonexistent.

Lucinda wore perpetually a heavy brown woolen coat, several inches too short in the arms, opening in the front to reveal a huge, hard swell of breast, which, like large iron balls, rolled within the thin material of her blouse. Her skirt, which was a charcoal brown in most places—various colors elsewhere—hung bedraggled to her mighty slabs of thigh.

Lucinda rolled up her coat sleeve to scratch at her massive arm.

Lucinda also stole the linens.

At that particular moment, Lucinda had been tucking one of the tablecloths into the opening of her coat. She looked at Uncle darkly.

"What tablecloth?" she said.

She whipped the tablecloth deftly out of her dress bosom

and crammed it into the drawer. She picked up the doily off the bureau and stuffed it in the front of her coat.

Uncle looked up. "What, Mrs. Turncew?"

I slipped into one of the big chairs in the parlor and started to systematically stuff the shredded remains of a Baptist pamphlet down under the fat, stained cushion. I chewed on my fingertips.

Mrs. Turncew opened her mouth and then shut it—she sounded like a fish drowning in air. She smiled at him and gave a flutter of her old, parched eyelashes. I wondered if they would break off.

"Don't you think we've been neighbors," she stressed the word as if to point up the irony, "long enough so that *you* might call *me* Nellcine?"

Lucinda waddled over to the buffet—which indeed was more like some squatting animal than a piece of furniture, equipped as it was with clawed feet, and crawling with tiny knots and bulges, and several eagle drawer pulls that Mrs. Winslow had painted mauve in her pink period. She gave it a perfunctory swat, seized the doily that lay upon it, and scuttled off to her cubicle.

Uncle leaned back. Artistically he tucked a piece of rubbery fat back into the hole in his T-shirt from which it had crept to peer at the world. "No," he said.

Mrs. Turncew's face collapsed into a whole maze of sagging wrinkles, one following in the other's wake, not unlike dominoes, so that she resembled an Austrian shade. She wiped at her nose.

"And now, dear lady," said Uncle, heaving himself out of the chair in which he had been residing, "it's out to the chicken coop and the raw February winds that I go." He swung his belly toward the back door. He strode forth.

"Oh, but Lamb!" cried Mrs. Turncew. "I wish you wouldn't go out there! The air just can't be healthy! Why! I . . . Don't you at least want some hot soup?"

The door slammed.

Mrs. Turncew fell back on her heels. She reached up under her dress and pulled her garters down.

I watched her from the darkness where I sat.

Mrs. Turncew was a rather dim woman. She was dressed always in muted, colored nylon crepe, old-lady dresses. She was a splash of blue and green and orange and red, or yellow and brown, or pink and white and maroon. The dresses were all of the same cut. They fell across a flat bosom and hit her below the knees, almost to her swollen and pear-shaped ankles. This was not to say that Mrs. Turncew didn't have a bosom. She had one, all right, but long use and, no doubt, sleeping on her stomach had mashed it to the point where now, in her fifty-sixth year, it hung oblivious to the brassiere that was supposed to give it new life and vim, but merely kept it intact. It seemed to me then that, if released, her bosom would blow to powder.

Her waist billowed about her like chiffon.

Her hair was a sort of mouse-brown, interwoven with great chunks of silver, the varying colors of alloy. It rolled from a wide—steadily widening—part in the middle of her head; lay flat in distinct, chunky strands; and became, at the juncture of her head and spine, and the line designated by her ears, round and incredibly saucy gray sausage curls.

To lend symmetry to the incredible apparition above her ears, Mrs. Turncew wore the most fascinating and terrifying earbobs that I have yet to see.

There was a pair of monstrous pine cones, swallowing her ears with their size, and frosted as if with snow.

On that day she wore a pair of powder-blue globes the size of golf balls, punctuated at frequent intervals by large clusters of spikes, their deadliness sheathed in glitter. They were fully an inch long, and diabolically pointed.

Her features were muddy—it seemed as if she were a turned-over jello mold that had lain in the refrigerator too long. Her features had melted. Grown fat with their loss of form, they were indistinct in this, the darkest room of the house.

Mrs. Turncew looked out to where, in the twilight, I could see my uncle sitting on the chicken coop, his cigar in one hand, and what I knew must be a beer can hidden in the folds of his stomach. The air was heavy with the beads of a chill gray rain that clung to the window and made his body seem a waving, watery memory thing.

I slowly opened my hand and looked at a locket that I had found deep and buried in dust at the bottom of a hand vase in his room. I passed my finger over the outer cover of it; it caught against the tiny etching, the scratches that shot across its ancient surface. I tried to open it with the end of my fingernail, but it remained closed. I knew it was hers, though —the first Emmeline's. There was an E initialed in its corner, and a glint of burnished hair which poked out of the inside of it. I shut my eyes and imagined the picture—a girl, dressed in a white middy blouse. The hand pressed to her breast would be covered with diamonds.

Mrs. Turncew picked up some pans and, slapping an entire array of kitchenware onto the stove, began to make soup.

CHAPTER *Four*

I was eight before I first saw a map of Indiana.

I had gone through the first grade, the second grade, the third grade—in that order, and each with the same teacher, the fragile and ancient Mrs. Bird. Mrs. Bird was sixty-three.

In a fit of pique eight years before, Mrs. Bird had taken down the map of Indiana and shellacked it to her lampshade. I never set foot across Mrs. Bird's formidable threshold. Her apartment squatted atop the Eli Lilly warehouse in a singularly dark and sinister manner, thrusting numerous tongues of plastic purple orchids out at the world at large via canary-yellow window boxes. According to those few who had seen the place, the lampshade was still there. The map had been, before its truncation, a tad longer than the lampshade was round. Mrs. Bird had coped admirably with this by cutting off certain portions of lower Indiana, an act which, for the first time in recorded history, created the meeting of Delphi and Gary, thereby rendering the map anatomically unsound.

Due to a lack of information, I had always imagined Indiana as looking like Texas. The shape of the latter reposed on the Falstaff beer cans that were my uncle's joy and solace, adorning his large and horny-hided hand one minute, and in the next retiring to a crowd of empties that sat where once chickens had been meant to roost—inside my Grandfather Lamb's chicken coop.

The shape had first impressed me when, rummaging through a vast reservoir of empties, I had chanced upon a little light by which to ascertain that indeed this was not rust but some rune that the Falstaff bottling company had embossed upon their product, designed to convey some dark and otherwise interesting message.

I asked Uncle. He eyed it closely; then, having determined in his mind that it was indeed this, he pronounced to me that the mysterious symbol was a state, just which one didn't matter.

The stars on the flag all looked the same, I knew, and each star, I rationalized, was intended to represent a state; therefore, with the one exception of the state represented by the star that Rocky Freshower had drawn over with a cross and skull on Armistice Day, it took little to conclude that all the states must look alike, and therefore like the state on the Falstaff beer can.

One day Uncle showed me, from a book he had, a map of Indiana.

It stretched from Lake Michigan in the north to the heel of Kentucky, meeting the hills of that state in jagged lines. Looking at the map of Indiana, watching my uncle trace the eccentric lines of it, now straight, taut, unreal, now breaking into riotous curves and angles, with his fat finger—pink in this light, and cased in a hide of leather—I memorized his hands. His fingers were creased, a stern, horny maze of indentations, almost like a thousand tiny wrinkles. Yet inside—I could almost see inside the hard, slick coating—they seemed soft, as pliable and slightly, sweetly moist as a tiny child's.

I would feel his finger with mine, and the jaggedness of it would catch on my skin and pull at it—the ragged places where the cuticle gave birth to a scarred and blunt yellow fingernail, the rough standing-up places at his knuckles.

He would drag it heavily down the map, painfully almost, as if with his finger he could feel and touch and smell and even hear the music of the people who lived in that town.

The map would be damp behind and, with the oil that flowed from his finger, faintly yellow.

The White River was a broad one. The distance between its banks was wide, almost as wide as the Wabash up around Lafayette, broad enough so that you could see to the other side and the trees looked smaller.

Uncle knew a lot about the White River. He said once that he had grown up along it. He hadn't. But he had been to Turkey Run once, for three days. We had a pillow—satin, bright, China-blue—and on it was embroidered the observation "I've been to Turkey Run," and the picture of a spare, running turkey, the wind behind in yellow and green. I figured that going to Turkey Run was just about as good as living on the White, it being on the White as it was.

The White was in the central part of the state, down in the magical limestone country, where the hills were purple-green, sometimes even blue, and rocks sprang up from the soil to point at the sky. The land was crossed and crossed again, laced in a network of shallow, ankle-deep streams that ruminated gently over thousands of bright-colored, speckled, smooth rocks. Some of them, Uncle said, looked like little gray frog eyes, all shiny and flecked and somehow alive, which stared at you from the clear water bottom of the tiny streams.

He had seen a flower once, he said, fragile and bright, orange and speckled and striped, lifting its cup and drinking from one long and extended tear of a minute waterfall.

At Turkey Run the hills were pierced with thousands of caves, narrow, not good dwelling-caves, but good shimmying-through caves. They were formed, Uncle said, by water. They smelled damp and almost chemical, and their walls were red mud. Lizards hung all bright and green on the walls. They were dark and small.

Outside, the White was met by brown mud beaches. All the mud that had denied itself to the countless small streams met here, on the mightier river's banks, and anxiously awaited its turn to plummet into the already swift-running brownness.

At times, when the only sound was the quiet and constant drone of the currents running underneath the surface, and the butterfly flight of leaves brushing in an early noon's sun, if you were careful to watch, you could get the paw mark or the spidery imprint of a bird's hesitant foot. You dug it out of the mud and filled it with plaster. In an hour or so you would have a fine and dirty model of the print.

With his fingers Uncle traced the White as it spread to meet with the Wabash. He picked out the Tippecanoe. With his finger he searched for the Eel, the Salamonie, the Mississinewa. He traced the wanderings of Wild Cat Creek.

"These here," he said, "drain the north and central parts of the state. And this one here, the White, now, not the White-water, the *White,* that one drains the southern part. The White ends just above us. Top of Posey County."

There was limestone, Uncle said, all across the southern part of the state, a remnant of a faraway time when the hairy elephants called mammoths first lay down in the snow to begin their thousand-year sleep.

Niagara limestone, Hamilton Limestone. And under the hills lay coal, soft and chalky to the touch, gray-brown, dully colored. And beneath all of it—the limestone, the coal—lay the dark and nightlike bubblings of oil fastened deep in the earth.

With his finger he traced the Wabash in its flow, traced it down the map, through the towns—through Wabash, Lafayette, Delphi, to its meeting with Illinois, to its merging with the Ohio.

Chaucy lay cradled in the big toe of the state, nestled deep within the crotch of the combined rivers, the Wabash and the Ohio.

On the bluff behind the factory, I would stand in the vibrant light of late afternoon with the grass licking at my feet in the water breeze, and watch the two rivers as they met.

The Ohio is a river of purpose. It rushes—red-brown, its pigment stolen from under the watchful eyes of its German farmers—to meet, finally, with the Mississippi, where, with the decisiveness that has marked it from its hill source to its water grave, it promptly gives up the ghost.

The Wabash is not made of such stern stuff. It is born from God knows where, and meandering aimlessly along, humming a tuneless song in summer, stopping dead still in winter, by some miracle of gravity and osmosis it winds its way down to the vicinity of Southern Indiana in general, the vicinity of Chaucy in particular and, with the vagueness which has characterized its journey from birth to innocuous death, limps to merge with its more vigorous fellow.

But it never compromised.

The Wabash may have shared the same riverbed with the Ohio, but it shunned its company. The Ohio ran. The Wabash walked and swung its parasol to unheard songs. From the footwalk of the Candlemar Section Bridge, from the factory bluff, I could see the line where one river ended and another started up. They never melted together. They most certainly never compromised.

For a hundred years, or nearly that, people had waded in the river's fork. They chose mysteriously the Wabash side.

The Wabash had a smell to it—the smell of limestone, of mud, the acrid smell of cornfields and the northern hog farms, a smell almost chemical, strong, familiar. Its mud was the mud of Indiana, its soil washed down from the dank and clammy banks and smelling high of decay. It was a suspicious river, wary. Its moods were calculable, as slow and insolent as the catfish that slid silver-smooth and evilly whiskered through the yellow and thick film of river water.

In the late afternoon I would walk down the hill made rough with small brown rocks and the shells of river animals, and crawl to sit on Cling On Rock, so called because Louise

Kelperman hadn't one day, and, it being a river and she being a girl and some eight months pregnant, had sunk to a watery grave, only to rise again on the Fourth of July, the day after which, her somewhat soggy dust was returned to earth in the graveyard the other side of Beekerman's Hill.

I would sit on its mud-slick surface, above a small finger of loam that stretched into the face of the river and was the bearer of many millions of tiny gray shells, and minute snails, drab and slimed if they moved.

The Ohio had too much of a nervous clip to it. It is a river with bug eyes. It sputtered. It gasped for air. Its voice was shrill, high, its feet ever running, and the rocks you offered up to it were swallowed in an insistent and a greedy way.

Cling On Rock was the season-watching place.

When winter with her icicles colored the fingered trees with silver, and all that could be heard in the white and silent world was the tinkling of ice as soft winds played among the trees, faraway and musical—like the cry of a faery in the snow —I would come to Cling On Rock and sit atop its chill and slightly slick surface. This porous surface was colored dark with accumulated moisture. The sound of my rocks hitting on the rearing heads of ice that grew along the side of the sluggish river were the only sounds in a world of no sound.

In winter's silence I would leave the world of the river, with its pathetic and glassy-surfaced trees bending to cast only dim and muted shadows on the crags of ice that the river cast up, and its bugs frozen within icicles an eighth of an inch thick.

I left it, scaled the muddy bank, crossed the meadow of marshy and gray blowing grass, reached Nation Street, and began to climb back up into the town. The bridge crept across the river like a beaver with its gray and angular body. I walked down Marley to Jean Street.

It was ugly, Chaucy was. It rose small and square, and its

houses on the slightly rolling hills were like cinder boxes. To the north the land swelled and bubbled into the hills, and then stretched to become the first hint of northern cornfields, colored heat-yellow in the Midwestern sun, and hog farms with their arid smell of crusted mud and pig flesh.

To the south it billowed, and in this season its hills were alive with the moving of tall, dry grass, gray in the gray of sky.

Chaucy stood high on the river's bluff. The town was shaped in a way reminiscent of an arrowhead, meeting at a point and flanked by the two rivers meeting below this highest point.

The River Road ran around the town. It began on the Wabash side and, rounding the point, ran along the Ohio side and up into Delphi, to Kokomo, clear through to the cool of Ohio shade trees.

Up the Wabash side of the River Road climbed Nation Street, which reached the crest of the town just a little below the factory adorning Chaucy's highest point, then continued downward on the opposite side until it met with the River Road again, this time on the Ohio side.

We lived on Jean Street, which was in the older section of town, built in the first days of its settlement, and in the shadow of the great factory.

From our house you could see the River Road, which, like a length of gray ribbon let fall over the land, wove on and on into the east. Facing the road stood house upon farmhouse, tall, almost like roots half pulled from loam. Faded houses with sagging porches, and shutters lying in heaps before the narrow barn, and signs still nailed into the hoary hide of an ancient oak tree: "Buy your vegetables HERE," blown with winter wind. I remembered the days when, a few months before, a young boy with red hair and cut-down overalls had "watched" the stand. Squash, pumpkins, peppers covered with dust, apples, speckled pears. A weather vane hanging haphazardly, and by one leg, to the spindle on which it once revolved. And now the river, and the ice.

Jean Street branched off from Nation, turned a corner and became Marley, turned another corner and became Lee Ambrose Avenue, turned another and became Milk, and then became Jean again. In reality these streets—Jean, Marley, Lee Ambrose, and Milk—were only fingers of streets, not long enough to be considered more than lanes; and Milk, indeed, was actually a part of Nation, becoming Milk only for the space of one short block before it became Nation again. Together they enclosed a perfect square, an area so small that it could only contain four houses, one at each of the corners.

Our house stood on the corner of Jean and Marley, and was separated from Mrs. Larbuck's house—squatting gracelessly on the corner of Milk and Jean—by only a foot-or-so-wide stretch of tall grass, and the various debris behind the chicken coop.

Mrs. Larbuck's house was large and tall, nearly three stories tall if you counted the somewhat limited space under her attic beams. The house was composed of huge, damp, brown blocks, which sat upon each other in such a way that they constructed a very admirable, very ugly square, providing a base for her peaked tin roof to crouch upon. Said roof was abloom with the geraniums that her maiden daughter, Elsie, teetered up to water and prune each morning. Elsie would stand, wrapped only nominally in a wild and faded blue housecoat, which seethed around her bony ankles like some tangible sea, and was the cause of many a potted geranium's tragic descent to death three stories below. Stark against the light of early morning she would stand, her features dimmed, her outline frank and angular. With small and cautious thrusts of the thin, nozzle-like stem of her watering can, she doused the geraniums.

The house was completely surrounded on the bottom story with a porch composed of the same hideous blocks that distinguished its walls. It was here—hidden by numerous dark and woolly flora, a couple of chains of a heavier sort, and randomly situated tires, of which Mrs. Larbuck's departed husband had been a salesman—that Mrs. Larbuck was able to make her morning promenade, visible only to the various fruit flies sharing her abode and, of course, to her daughter, whose years in the darkness of the musty house had widened her eyes until they were quite large, as compound as the flies' own.

On the corner of Lee Ambrose and Marley stood Mrs. Turncew's home. It was small, one story, possessed of a porch whose screen thwarted sight into, and whose front door revealed, the bathroom, equipped with a small and ancient toilet. Mrs. Turncew's house was dark. The furniture was plump and hard; its shiny, slick chintz, the color unrecognizable in the lack of light, was cold and slippery. On each table, on each mantle or bureau or muffin cabinet, squatted colored and cut-glass canisters which bloomed with every sort of stale confection and candy and pecan cracker imaginable, together with dimestore-framed pictures of her husband, her sisters, her mother, and Clark Gable. There were doilies, I remember, everywhere, on every chair, so insecure that with the slightest provocation they would slide winging down the furniture. Stale music, sodden with must, poured out of an ancient standing, domed radio in a thick and constant stream.

On the corner of Lee Ambrose and Milk stood the Fosbrink house.

It had been, in its time, a very fine house. It was narrow in the way of the canal house, white after a fashion, and the shingled roof, which had once risen proud and steep into the air, was now denuded of its shingles—for the most part due to the efforts of Mrs. Fosbrink, who peeled them off the roof with a hammer, painted Bible scenes on the back of them, and hung them in her kitchen.

The Fosbrinks' porch remained standing only through the whim of God.

[2 9

There remained only two unbroken windows. Due to the fact that Mrs. Fosbrink, an active homemaker, had once decided she wanted a brick walk, the chimney was rapidly sinking into the roof.

The other house on the square belonged to the Roses. Their house was dark and small, constructed after the manner of Mrs. Turncew's house, possessed of walls of different sizes of rocks, ranging from boulders to pebbles, slicked over and damp with the drab green that infects everything in southern Indiana in the winter.

Such was our neighborhood, small and square, an island of four houses. Across the street lived the Freshowers. Down the street lived the Maces. Nearby lived the Penicks. Between and among and around them lived all manner of old ladies and men, all with names, all looking alike, their faces hidden perpetually in the darkness that characterized their tiny homes. I knew their names then. I don't now.

I would stop at the crest of Nation and look down, over the town.

The sun had beat down on it for ninety years' time. It had been conceived by Homer Milk, born a canal town in the mind of this enterprising New Yorker in the year 1846. Milk, having inherited the care of his blind nephew, arrived in what was to become Chaucy by dint of foot and theft of horse in the spring of that year. He married an Indian maiden named Miranda Big Moose. He successfully guided his nephew down the paths of the forest wood. In November he appeared in Buffalo, consulted some friends, who consulted some friends in turn. Eventually, after much consultation, some friend of a friend had a rich friend, and the Kentucky Star Canal was born.

The Erie Canal was in its prime. But neither it nor its less famous but profitable offshoot, the Wabash and Erie, which dallied along the shores of the sleepy-running Wabash, touched the south of the state.

Canals caused towns to spring up and swell to reach the sky in twisted towers, to abort light, thrusting it through the colors of stained-glass windows brought on barges. They brought bizarre lamps and square grand pianos and false electric logs that burned blue in the false fireplaces of the great mansions. Mansions rose around them, modeled after Italian villas integrated with certain aspects of Notre Dame. Indiana cried out, in well-modulated tones, its pride and importance. Its towns crouched in state by the man-made rivers of America's frontier.

Homer knew. He had watched the explosion of wealth brought in on the west-bound barges of the canals. He had passed with wonder through the tree-shaded, bricked streets of Delphi. He had walked along the brick sidewalks on Canal Street in Lafayette, caught in the shadows of the massive houses that the waterways, with their commerce, had given rise to. He saw the tall canal houses, narrow, red with brick or wood painted dusky maroon. They were crowned with turrets, towers. Their stairwells were lighted always by a small triangle-topped square of stained glass. Their doors shut heavy, carved. Their doorknobs shone dully in dim light, and sound . . . sound revolved like velvet skirts, swirling thick and soft with silence. They hid behind their mellowed whisperings all the mystery, all the excitement, all the change and desperation of a people trying to stuff a brief, fast, fleeting miracle with all the realized dreams that they could. He walked in the streets of these glory-struck towns.

It was the canal that brought the wealth, but the true wealth lay in the cities that would spring from its sides. Homer bought the land around Chaucy, a stretch of country encompassing almost ten miles of unsettled territory. He had figured on everything. He had the land. He had the backers. He had the equipment. He had the engineers. He had the route all planned out, starting from the Atlantic in upstate Virginia, traveling through that state, through Kentucky to

Indiana's southwesternmost point. He had figured on everything. . . .

Except the Appalachian Mountains.

The Kentucky Star was shelved for technical reasons.

Homer had quite a problem on his hands. Overnight, people had flocked to "Milktown"; tents gave way to crude homes; crude homes gave way to the scaffoldings of finer homes. Homer took a long look at the boom town he had created, a long look at the boom which had just deflated, and he did the only sensible thing left to do—he died.

For three months the scaffolding froze in the winter sky. Then Johann Chaucy, weary of scraping his living off the fertile topsoil of Ohio, took his small family to Milktown and opened a livery shop on the point of land where the factory now stands. When he had accumulated enough capital from his livery shop, he opened the first corseting factory in Indiana. Within a reasonable number of years, Johann, cursed with an overfondness for things of the flesh, most specifically the flesh of young women, died ghoulishly, at the age of fifty-three, of syphilis.

His son, Turth, took it over. In 1878, he turned it into a contraceptive factory in memory of his father's ignominious demise.

After which it enjoyed a brief career as a dirty-toy factory, merrily rolling out obscene balloons and other nasties until 1928, when Turth's three heirs, satiated with wealth, sold the factory to an order of nuns and betook themselves to the Sodom of St. Paul, to live out their lives of sin in luxury and happiness.

The sisters turned the factory into a hospital—St. Stephen's, by name. But, finding the Chaucites devoid of any maladies more excruciating than terminal gas and full of denunciations for Popes and Papists in general, the good ladies also betook themselves to St. Paul, in search of plague victims and adequate funds.

Chaucy's history was reflected in the walls of the factory. It stands, its windows darkened, its huge and massive bulk framed by the sun as it sets. Its west façade is a moving surface of water reflection.

But Chaucy was born a canal town. Cheated of its dream, it hides its face behind the flat and Victorian façades of its houses. It says to a world that knows better, "I am moving. My water runs a clear thing, uncovered by algae. This green you see is only temporary."

Ninety years. Winter's cold had softened its lines. The sweet, faintly green rain of spring had lain in its cracks and carved out its memory. Now it stood mellow in the faint golden light that seeped through winter's cloud. It rested quiet on its river bluff where shaggy trees cast their shadows. It rested quiet in the memory of its clear color, clean in the stained brass of its door handles, in the tuneless tones of the broken pianos that, like birds, caught on a cushion of air. The sunlight wove through it in channels of gold.

CHAPTER *Five*

Mrs. Turncew took up residence in our kitchen as of February and was, in this, the early time, putting her hand to various tentative and trivial tasks—an occasional batch of woebegone cookies, a platter of bloated confections.

Uncle stalked the house like some caged animal. He snuck furtively back to the chicken coop whenever her lumpy and nylon-sheathed back was turned, to sit in his chair and, softly, because of his fear of discovery, curse the weather. These moments of bliss were few and far between. Upon sight of Uncle's huge body seated in pontifical, intimidated splendor atop the chicken coop, Mrs. Turncew would seize a massive sweater that had once housed the formidable belly of her first husband, and a plate abloom with flat, despairing delicacies, and hotfoot it out to the back yard. She would attack him alternately with sweater and banal confections. For Mrs. Turncew was possessed of that power to know when you are cold even when you yourself do not realize it. She would swat Uncle Lamb with the sweater, then force a cookie down his unwilling throat, and by sheer main force wrest him off the chicken coop to sit with her in the dining room. Uncle stood it for as long as he could. Then he began seeking other refuges. He locked himself in the pantry. She stuck the broom handle under the door, whose casing was abnormally low, and batted it around until he went up into the attic. She decided the attic needed cleaning. He locked himself in his room, and she decided that the woodwork needed repainting. Telling Mrs.

Turncew "no" was impossible. She followed him everywhere. Through keyholes she peered at him, around corners she lurked, waiting for him, under doors she slid messages and cookies. There was only one place where Uncle was free of Mrs. Turncew—the bathroom.

It was when they brought the coffin in that Uncle went into the bathroom and didn't come out.

Mrs. Turncew had long been convinced that her dentist husband would survive her in life. When he had, upsetting her plan, kicked the bucket so prematurely, Mrs. Turncew was beset with a problem. There was one thing that vitally worried her—now that Marshall was dead, who would pick out her coffin when she died?

Mrs. Turncew knew in her mind that she could not bear to be laid to rest in any but the best coffin. The very thought of eternity spent in an inferior model dismayed her—it kept her awake nights. Finally she hit upon the perfect solution.

One day she went to Boxwright Brothers' Funeral Supply and Co-operative and, after a space of some two and a half hours—which Uncle, freed from the sweater and the cookies and her grappling, heavy-veined hands, spent atop the chicken coop—settled on a coffin.

I remember it quite well. It was the best and the most exotic that Boxwright Brothers' had in stock, as well it should have been. It weighed many more pounds than it should have, and was composed of a walnut tree split in two, it seemed, and then joined by small square wedges of the same wood at the end. It was, like the original tree, curved, coming to rest at the bottom in a flat and much-adorned base which was resplendent with drawer pulls, of the Greco-Roman fashion, to which there were no drawers.

The oiled, shined, and incredibly polished curve of thick wood that was born from the base also crawled with drawer pulls. Their brass base was square and plain except for a raised rim; the drawer pull was a round ring.

The coffin was lined with plush black satin, quilted in the manner of the canopy on Mrs. Turncew's bed. It gave me the idea that she was just boning up for her days in eternity.

The coffin also had a music box hidden somewhere within its deep chambers that solemnly tolled out "The Consecrated Cross I'd Bear" for eternity—or at least that portion of it included in the five-year guarantee.

I was sitting in the foyer, dropping marbles down the radiator, when I first heard the hearse pull in.

Through the icebound and silent streets it came, loping in the manner of all hearses, holding its black top hat against the wind, its mouth weighted at the corners, its window glass dewy with sympathy. It churned and fermented until it tumbled into a standstill in front of our porch walk, and then— with a solemn lurch, like a hiccup caught in mid-flight—it stopped.

I stood up and stuffed my underwear into my pants. "Hearse's here," I said. I scratched my stomach.

Miss Tibbitt looked concernedly about the room, her watery eye falling on each one of us. "Is anyone here dead?" she asked. She glanced again at Miss Kitty. Then, tentatively, she touched herself.

"They're getting out," I said.

"Who?" asked Mrs. Logg.

"Mr. Boxwright," I said. I gave up on my underpants, and unzipped my jeans and crammed them in. "And the other Mr. Boxwright. And Mrs. Turncew."

"Is she alive?" demanded Miss Rama, gathering up her old knees and bounding gleefully for the window.

"Seems to be," I said.

Miss Rama turned back to the room, her face downcast. "That certainly is a relief," she mumbled. She sat down and struck her knees together.

"They're bringing something else out," I said. "Of the

wagon. It's . . ." I pulled the flimsy and sooty little curtain away from the window. "It's a coffin."

"Is anybody *in* it?" screamed Miss Rama, frenzied with joy. She began to collect her limbs for another assault on the window.

"There's a podium in it," I said. "There's a book." I whistled. "Geeze in the morning, that sure is a big coffin!"

It was a big coffin.

Mr. Boxwright staggered under its front weight, and the elder Mr. Boxwright stumbled along behind him, his end of the coffin sinking in his straining hands. It dipped and swayed with his movement.

Mrs. Turncew scurried alongside the coffin, tapping it occasionally, making small talk with the struggling but ever-courteous funeral directors, who, reeling from side to side, smiled and nodded in a very silent and knowing way.

Thusly did the procession ramble about the front yard, veering to the left and falling back to the right. Through the windowpane in the door, I could see the elder Mr. Boxwright, taller than his brother, grin, his eyes veiled, and I saw his lips form the studied "oops" that only a funeral director can manage when he makes some gruesome mistake. This went on for fifteen minutes.

Eventually the front door was attained. Mrs. Turncew leaped to it merrily and pushed it open; the coffin made its gay and swinging way into our narrow hall, accompanied by more studied "oopses" from the elder Mr. Boxwright as he slammed into walls, gouged tables, and made sharp-ended and stabbing thrusts at the soft bodies of the ladies.

Mr. Boxwright the elder, who was, as I have said, taller than young Mr. Boxwright, seemed like a piece of taffy stretched out to dry—long, thin, and brittle, all his fibers running upwards. He had the flattest mouth that I have ever seen. It sprang from nowhere on his face and extended matter-of-factly and perfectly horizontally across the middle of his face; then, like some Eli Lilly factory worker, it punched its timecard and left. This mouth he elevated in his face for a smile; when he frowned from sympathy it dropped down to his jaw, remaining all the time horizontal.

But it was the eyes of Mr. Boxwright the elder that I remember best. Beneath his cap of sparse and wettish black hair, painfully combed over that portion of his head already depopulated, locked under his overhanging eave of wrinkled brow, were Mr. Boxwright's eyes. Even in the shadow cast by his massive forehead, they were arresting in their paleness. His face a geometrical pattern, his eyes were round, huge, and bulbous. The irises were large and pale, lacking in any dark spot; fluidly they swam from place to place on his vast orbs, and yet, because of the lack of a pupil, it was impossible to tell where he was looking. Right then he cast his eyes on me, as you might cast a fishing bait. The horizontal line of his mouth moved upward.

Young Mr. Boxwright was almost the opposite of his brother. Five years the junior, young Mr. Boxwright was small and quite round, possessed of a sparse red fuzz which covered his head, and a large, fat, and meaty red tongue that swam out of his mouth, drooped over the corners of it, and captured air. Young Mr. Boxwright also stuttered.

Messieurs Boxwright stood swaying—half in the front hall, half in the parlor.

Mr. Boxwright the elder drew in his eyes and then, turning, cast them out to the ladies, who by this time had risen from their chairs and armed themselves with fans.

Mrs. Turncew patted the coffin so firmly that it bounced in the undertakers' hands. She smiled brightly.

"Good afternoon, ladies," exuded Mr. Boxwright the elder. His voice was limpid with sympathy, soft and insidious as a brook threatening flood. "Brother Norton and I have just stopped by to deliver a little . . . item to your home. We trust it will not have to be used for a long, long time." A pale fire burned in his eye. His horizontal line elevated itself until it touched the bottom of his spare nose.

"Ah-ah-ah-ah-ah-ahmamamen," said Brother Norton. He reached up with his muscular tongue and licked the beads of sweat off his face.

"Why, Nellcine," said Miss Tibbitt, pointing her fan at the coffin. "It's just lovely, dear. When did you get it?"

"Right this day," said Mrs. Turncew. Once again she patted it violently. The Boxwright brothers dove to catch it.

"And now, dear madame," said Boxwright the elder, "where . . . ?" He lifted his right hand delicately and waved it quizzically over the room. The coffin, supported only by three hands, went into a sharp decline. Mr. Boxwright the elder grabbed it. From where I was standing I could see perspiration rise suddenly to his forehead; then, suddenly mindful, it folded its hands and retired back into his pores.

Mrs. Turncew favored the parlor with a sweeping glance. "Right . . ." She sucked on her tangled, veined hand. "Right . . . there! There!" She pointed to a relatively empty area under the west window.

"Righto," said the elder Mr. Boxwright urbanely. He smiled sympathetically at her.

With a grand swinging of coffin, the brothers Boxwright escaped violent contact with the hall wall—an action which, if consummated, would have led to the untimely discorporation of our house. They careened into the parlor, barely missing furniture, the stuffed chickens that formed the mainstay of our lamps, and the urns.

"Oops," said Boxwright the elder ghoulishly. He leered at Mrs. Turncew.

At the back of the house I heard a door slam, and turning, I saw Uncle Lamb walk into the room. He stopped. He looked at the coffin. He looked at Mrs. Turncew. He looked quickly back into the coffin to make sure that she wasn't in it. He stalked back out the door.

"Oh, Lamb," trilled Mrs. Turncew, running after him in mincing steps and seizing him by the sleeve of his T-shirt, "come see what I bought!"

The elder Mr. Boxwright pulled the podium out of the coffin.

It was immense and carved with some regard to eternity. On its oily and time-darkened body there resided innumerable angels, each of them armed with two wings and two harps, and allotted one cloud on which he perched. The rest of the carving consisted of a sort of mahogany edelweiss.

Mrs. Turncew, the large and rubbery hoses of her veins standing at attention under her transparent film of skin, dragged Uncle over to the coffin.

"Now this, Mr. Lamb . . ." Boxwright the elder indicated the podium, at that moment still rising from the coffin like some startled phoenix, "is a podium." His voice was soft and sympathetic, almost subliminal. "When the beloved dead is set into the coffin . . ."

Brother Norton rolled creepily around the room, scraping the furniture and then examining his fat finger for dust. I looked at him. I drew my finger over the muffin table. I looked at it.

"What do you mean, bringing a coffin into my house?" demanded Uncle in a low whisper to Mrs. Turncew. "Who's dead? Who?"

Boxwright the elder elevated his line up to under his nose and went on just as softly and as soothingly as before, ". . . God rest her dear soul . . . and your kind friends, your dear neighbors flock to you in your Hour of Grief. . ."

"Now, Lamb," said Mrs. Turncew. "Don't get so *excited*. It's only a cautionary thing. I might not die for, oh, fifteen or twenty years. . . ."

4 0]

". . . you'll want to remember them, each and every one of them; and so we at Boxwrights' want you to have the very love-liest of craftsmanship for the podium on which . . ." With his long and spidery hand he dragged out a large gold-leaved book, on which was emblazoned the word "Departure." ". . . this guest book!"

Brother Norton coyly took a swat at one of the chicken lamps. It glowered at him through two pop-beads of eyes.

"You've got a house of your own!" shouted Uncle Lamb. He struggled to free himself from her grip. He reached up and unpried her hand. "Why don't you take your coffin over to *your* house?"

Boxwright the elder reverently pulled the podium com-pletely out of the coffin and set it upright.

"Oooh," said the ladies at the edelweiss.

"Now here we have . . ." oozed Boxwright the elder. He stopped. Here we had a large black plaque which stated "Property of Boxwright Brothers' Funeral Supply and Co-op-erative." A strangled titter emerged from his pole of throat. He turned it around. "And here we have . . ."

"For God's sake, what are you going to *do* with the damn thing?!"

Miss Rama gasped and clapped her hands over my ears.

"Mr. Lamb!" she exclaimed. "How many times have I told you not when the child's . . ."

"But it's all terribly practical, Lamb . . ." began Mrs. Turn-cew.

"Edelweiss," cooed Boxwright the elder. "Beautiful Swiss edelweiss, and God's own angels . . ."

"Practical!" screeched Uncle Lamb. "Practical! What on earth could you . . ."

I unpried my ears from where they had been plastered to my head. I stuck my fingers in them to stop the ringing.

"To plant African violets in," said Mrs. Turncew.

Silence.

Boxwright the elder looked up from the podium, his face tumbled in consternation. "African violets . . ." he said. "But that's *satin!*" He waved his hands at the lining of the coffin.

"SaSsssasa . . ." Brother Norton gave up and sat down in the little armchair.

"Oh, don't worry," said Mrs. Turncew, turning to Boxwright the elder. "I'll put a plastic sack over the inside of it before putting any soil in."

Mrs. Logg peered at the west window. "Exposure's just right," she observed.

"But, I don't like African violets!" shouted Uncle Lamb.

"A good plastic bag. You're sure it'll be a good plastic bag?" asked Boxwell the elder, clinging to the edge of the coffin.

"I have just the thing," said Mrs. Turncew.

"Good and thick?"

"I don't like African violets!" screamed Uncle Lamb.

"If it's not good and thick . . ."

"It's from Marriannis's bed-wetting days."

"West," observed Mrs. Logg.

"I DON'T LIKE AFRICAN VIOLETS!"

"Why not?" asked the elder Boxwright. "Edelweiss is very nice, and see, it plays 'The Consecrated Cross I'd Bear.'" He leaned over and turned on something in the coffin. A mournful and slightly off-tune rendition of the hymn poured horizontally forth.

"The Constipated Cross-Eyed Bear?" I asked.

"*That does it!*" shouted Uncle Lamb. "*That does it! Here!* HERE!" He wrestled with his T-shirt. He yanked it out of his pants and tried to pull it off.

"May I help you with that?" asked Boxwright the elder, stepping urbanely forward and delicately laying his cold fingertips on Uncle's arm.

Uncle froze. Then he turned around and backed off. "No," he said. He held up his hand. "No." He took another step back. "Just stay where you are. All of you." I started to take a step toward him. "That means you, too!" he said.

I stuffed my underwear deeper into my jeans.

"Now," he breathed. "Now I am going, and I don't want any of you—hear, hear?—I-don't-want-any-of-you to try to stop me." With his hand held out and waving about him, he cut a line backwards through the ladies and out into the foyer. He reached the bathroom. He turned around and gave us one last look, then stepped in and turned the key. The sound of flushing filled the air.

CHAPTER *Six*

My Grandfather Lamb, having tired of women forever, entered the city limits of Chaucy for the first time one iridescent morning in early June 1906, while the witch of a sun, not yet having undergone her metamorphosis, still swam, like some plush and rich egg yolk, within the fragile bounds of her membrane.

I was told he left one wife in Marion. He left one wife in Kokomo. He left one wife in Ontario.

Similarly I was told he left one child in Marion, one child in Kokomo, one child in Ontario.

He brought with him thirty-two chickens and five tired roosters.

Grandfather built his farmlike house on Jean Street. His fowl friends occupied the forward portion of this uniquely structured building. He himself dwelt in the back regions.

The portion of the house that the chickens inhabited could have been likened to a front porch. It jutted out onto the lawn. It possessed steps leading down from it. It had a roof and posts with which it held that roof up. It had a porch swing. It had honeysuckle. It also had numerous clucking chickens, a good deal of chicken wire, and, through the years, what amounted to a very chicken-like smell.

The town matriarchs called Grandfather's chicken porch a disgrace. The relatives, of which there were two, called it a cubicle. Grandfather Lamb, being of a more practical turn of mind, called it a chicken coop.

Here he lived, sleeping on a West Point cot, eating eggs and an occasional jaundiced chicken, and indulging in his hobby of taxidermy. For Grandfather stuffed everything not alive in sight, until such time as he attained the age of sixty-nine. It was then that the minister of the First and only Congregational Church raised the point that, whereas Francis of Assisi had been a saint, Grandfather was a health hazard—and the chickens were condemned.

The ladies from the church came to get the chickens on a Saturday, the day before the fiftieth anniversary of the First Congregational Church—a celebration that featured, interestingly enough, a chicken supper—and dispatched them rather rapidly to heaven knows what hells.

Grandfather, upset by this distressing trend of affairs, and rapidly approaching senility, built a new, more orthodox chicken coop in the back yard, in the vain hope that his chickens might someday be returned to him.

After a week or so of sitting on the chicken coop and waiting, Grandfather fell off the roof and received multiple injuries, including a broken neck, that dispatched him somewhat rapidly to his death.

It was thus that the house came into the hands of Uncle Lamb's older brother, Floyd, the child spawned of that first wife in Marion.

Floyd used the chicken porch for his unlicensed hobby of dentistry, where he met his ghoulish death on the floorboards upon which chickens once trod. In the early spring of 1942, Floyd swallowed a prodigious amount of novocain, a deed that left him a somewhat cataleptic corpse. He was attempting to avoid the draft, which would have never fallen on Floyd anyway, as he was, at the time, well past what might possibly have been called his prime, and flatfooted.

It was only then, in '42, that the house fell to the ownership of my Uncle Lamb, who was the child that Grandfather had sired in Kokomo, and who, now in his middling years, was a shoehorn salesman in the central counties.

Perhaps it was only a whimsy of irony that Uncle chanced, four years afterwards, to think of his one remaining sibling, a woman born of the Ontario mother. I didn't know how Uncle knew of her. No one else in town seemed to have. But he took pains to find that younger sister, and when he did find her, he told me, he snatched what was to become my sainted mother out of that particular hovel over which she was hovering at that moment, and dragged her by main force to his father's house on Jean Street. This he had already turned into a boarding house for ladies of a delicate age, most of them so delicate that they faded off into death soon afterwards. The only one still living by the year I turned eight was Miss Kitty. My mother seems to have been his big mistake.

CHAPTER Seven

According to my uncle, my mother was, at the time she came to live with Uncle Lamb, rapidly approaching that dangerous age—not to be confused with that delicate age—for the most part because she was equipped with that dangerous visage: Mother was ugly and Mother knew it.

Mother was not yet washed up, but she knew she was going to be. She was more than concerned about it; she was ready for action.

In 1947, at a square dance, my mother met a young dairy farmer from Minnesota who had one blind eye and feet that, every few centimeters, sprang alive with a large and painful wart.

He allemanded right into her life, and just as quickly, allemanded left her with child, dos-à-dosing all the way up north to Minnesota as fast as his wart-infested feet and the Wabash Special could carry him.

In due time Mother delivered herself of me and, after giving the matter some thought, decided that I was simply a figment of her imagination. After saying as much to my uncle, she left to join "Arthur Murray."

"Arthur Murray" turned out to be that untrusty fellow, Death. In six weeks' time "Arthur Murray" had given my mother a severe case of ptomaine poisoning somewhere on the fishing coast of Oregon, and she was dispatched rather rapidly to her tomb.

Uncle, the one-time shoehorn salesman from Kokomo, was

now left with a household of women of a delicate age, and a figment of his sister's imagination.

He told me that he thought on the situation a while and decided that his sister's chosen way of thinking was a mature and rational one. He pronounced me a figment of *his* imagination as well, and proceeded to ignore me as best he could.

This evasion I rendered difficult by demonstrating a warm affinity for crying, and a love of such childish pranks as wetting my drawers as the spirit moved me.

Uncle condescended at last to naming me, discovering that my mother's practice of referring to me as "it" was highly impractical, the term "it" being applicable to so many individual and diverse things—the can opener, and the stuffed terrier, and Miss Kitty's gilt slop jar. With no little apprehension about the future, he wrote my name down on the birth certificate: Emmeline Lamb.

CHAPTER Eight

Uncle stayed in the bathroom until February was drawn up in its last breath. He emerged only for rare excursions up the stairs to sullenly retrieve some desired object, and for meals, through which he sat in a stony silence, methodically plucking the simulated fish eyes out of his broth—for a somewhat frivolous halibut that Grandfather had once fastened to a plaque above the end of the table had a habit of flinging out his glass eyes at inopportune moments.

Because of Uncle's steady attendance at meals, Mrs. Turncew moved in and seized total control of the cooking—an action which pleased Lucinda mightily, leaving her free as it did to slip about the house filching linens.

The ladies seemed to like Mrs. Turncew's cooking. I didn't. Neither did Uncle Lamb. She was overly fond of vegetables. She cooked them so long that, by the time dinner time had rolled around, they were completely exhausted. They limped from pan to plate and lay there, panting, white-hot to the tooth.

Mrs. Turncew prodded Uncle with her fork. "Eat it," she said. "It's good for you."

The vegetable, by this time indistinguishable, made no protest. It lay there and sweated, the damp beads of its perspiration sidling off of it and rolling about the plate.

Uncle would lift his fork gingerly from the table and pry the vegetable off the plate. Drunkenly it would roll to the other side of the plate. Meeting with the raised border, it would stop, and begin once more to cement itself to the plate. Mrs. Turncew also believed in well-cooked meat.

One had to flake the huge and irregular patches of burnt skin off the chicken. The toes of the beef were curled up and charred on the end. Pork chops were indistinguishable from the bone upon which their burnt flesh clung. All tasted rather chemical. It was as though part of the substance had already fled and joined with air.

Mrs. Turncew presided over this auto-da-fé with a jealous concern which rivaled Yahweh's selfish surveillance of the Hebrews. She used a well-aimed fork to steer the food to the mouth. By the time Uncle and I had reached the second despairing vegetable, she was a veritable fountain, spewing directives at us like a thousand droplets of water.

"The cabbage is good!" A command.

"The cauliflower is nutricious!" A threat.

The halibut joyously threw out his eyes. With gay abandon he dropped a fin down Uncle's back.

The ladies collapsed into conversation now and again; kicking each other's spare ankles under the table, they spilled sauce that spread in large white patches to join their ancient, porous flesh to the stuff of their dresses.

Lucinda padded in, in her scuffs, and stole the linen napkin from under Uncle's elbow.

Eventually Mrs. Turncew would dive into the smoky kitchen and bring forth the dessert: a bloated and crouching cake, a heavy and leering cake; parfaits which stared at one dismally from the base of filmy crystal cups; deflated pastries, their black entrails creeping out from narrow chasms in their doughy exterior mortars to surround their bodies in lugubrious and oily masses.

Mrs. Turncew at the table had the quickness and efficiency of a praying mantis. With lightning speed and a finicky precision, she would dart out and place yet another disgruntled biscuit on Uncle's plate, where it would stare at him so sullenly that in the end he was forced to eat it. With the same faster-than-the-eye-can-see hands she would douse his bowl with additional soup. Like the halibut, it had oily eyes that swam on its surface.

At length Uncle began to spend less and less time at his meals, which had hitherto been his greatest pleasure. Finally the night came when he didn't appear at all.

CHAPTER *Nine*

Mrs. Turncew sallied into the parlor and announced that dinner was sufficiently burnt to be placed on the table. Glancing in the direction of the bathroom, she delicately raised her voice so that it would carry through the thick panels that constituted the door.

No sound.

She hovered outside the door. She walked with small shuffling steps in front of it.

"Dinner," she trilled.

She looked at the door.

The door looked at her.

Mrs. Turncew, her eyes fastened always on the door, snuck over to where I was sitting on the hardwood foyer floor, pelting the radiator with marbles, and tapped me on the shoulder.

"Emmie," she said. She indicated the door with a slippage of her pupils on the large and glazed orbs of her eyeballs. "Could you please knock on the door and tell your Uncle that it's dinner time?"

I looked at Mrs. Turncew. I stuffed the underwear down into my jeans. I stood up. Then I knocked on the door. There was no answer.

"Dinner," I said.

"Dinner," I said again.

I looked at Mrs. Turncew. "He doesn't answer," I explained.

"Well . . ." Mrs. Turncew hopped off and onto the bottom step of the stairs. "Well, ask him why."

"Uncle," I said. "Why don't you answer?"

There came a dim rustle from the bathroom.

"I am making a stand."

"He's making a stand," I said to Mrs. Turncew.

"But . . . why?" Mrs. Turncew sprang from the first step to the second.

I sighed and turned to the door once more.

"Why?"

A deep and concentrated pause came from the bathroom.

"I am making a stand," said Uncle. "Bring my food in here. *You,* Emmeline."

I turned to Mrs. Turncew. "He said . . ."

"I heard what he said," said Mrs. Turncew, leaping from one step to the other in her frenzy. She clasped and unclasped her hands.

"Right now, Emmeline!" Uncle's voice was disembodied, faraway.

Mrs. Turncew drew up at once. It was not the command in the voice—there was none. Even if there had been, she had not absorbed the meaning of his words. Instead it was as if something had dawned on her. She stepped off the step decisively. She scurried off to the kitchen, saying crisply, "Emmeline, come in here and get your uncle some dinner."

I looked after her with wonder, and having stuffed back down under my jeans those hunks of underwear that crept and ballooned from my waistband like inflatable ghosts, I followed her.

CHAPTER *Ten*

I peered into the darkness of the living room. In the pale light I could see only the dim and lavender shapes of the four ladies as they gathered together at the small, selfish radiator. They were sheathed in the barest of light that sifted through winter's clouds, and filtered through the varied dirt and dust and microscopic plant life that our windows were dense with.

The parlor, as well as I can remember it, consisted of four corners, a thousand knickknacks, eleven urns, four stuffed chickens serving as bases for lampshades, and one moose head.

All the aforementioned corners were outfitted with what Miss Kitty coyly referred to as "corner catchalls." These "corner catchalls" were racklike constructions in full and florid Victorian design, fully equipped with arms reaching out, their fingers rich in the goo of gingerbread, to draw you in to examine their wares.

The ladies had been most conscientious. Whenever they received a gadget of some kind, whenever they attained, through devious means, a souvenir, the treasure was promptly and proudly displayed upon one of the "corner catchalls."

Seashells, huge, broken, pink, and slick inside. To the touch they were velvet, chipped in places. Holding them to your ear, you could hear the sound of the sea, Uncle said. I had never been to the sea. To me the seashell sounded magical, like walking down a big sewer pipe on a rainy day.

And there were cup-and-saucer sets informing the reader

that some old lady's daughter had been to Rock City in 1933 and had seen nine (count 'em) states.

Another feature of the "corner catchalls" was a fascinating collection of fans from all the major funeral homes in Southern Indiana—not to mention one from Delphi, one from Logansport, one from Gary, one from the Groce Funeral Home in Asheville, North Carolina, two from Louisville, one from Florence, South Carolina, and one from San Bernardino, California.

Ancient flowers gone to powdery straw with age, and old valentines sealed in wax paper. Candy boxes with a scattering of empty, brittle paper cups inside.

Huge jars filled with candy that had earned the description "stale" as many as five and six years before, rose from the shelves, their contents huddling low in the bottom of the jar, now stuck together until they resembled fish eggs.

Surveying all this and hanging in rare dignity over the false fireplace was the moose head.

Grandfather had bought the moose head immediately upon its detachment from moose, and, true to form, had stuffed it. He was somewhat less than successful.

In about a year the moose head began to lose its teeth. One by one, one at a time, Grandfather would find a tooth which the moose head had coyly let fall the night before.

Eventually what had remained to the moose throughout his life until his death, had been, in this, his more spiritual phase, cast by the moose head from him.

The teeth lay in a singularly yellow and decayed condition upon the carpet until such time as Grandfather emerged from his Thoreau period into his Rousseau period, whereupon he deposited the moose head's molars in the urn once frequented by Uncle Cobb, with the idea of someday making a necklace from them.

After having so gallantly distributed his teeth to the four

winds, the moose head felt called upon to shed some other portion of himself in similar manner. He kittenishly threw out an eyeball. (Grandfather, in taxidermy, took out the actual eyeball of his subject and put it in a leather trunk, which he kept sending to the sisters of St. Stephen's. They always sent it back. He used instead marbles that he bought at Amberson's. Depending on the specimen he was stuffing, the marble fit in the socket or it didn't.) The moose dropped another eyeball. These too were claimed by the urn where once was Uncle Cobb.

Next the moose head, exhilarated, indeed intoxicated by the great amount of attention that it was receiving from my grandfather—who, since he had stuffed him, had turned to chickens and Mrs. Larbuck's recently demised terrier puppy— gaily flung an antler. Just as gaily the antler shattered into a thousand pieces upon contact with Mater Terra, and was promptly vacuumed up.

The moose head, chagrined by this trend of affairs, abruptly ceased his wild discorporation of himself. That winter he still hung in the state in which my uncle had found him when he had first inherited the house, minus one antler, minus one set of teeth, minus one set of eyeballs.

That February Miss Tibbitt had been with us but a month and a little. It had been late December when she arrived, and the ground was hard with cold.

I sat on the hardwood floor of the foyer and absorbed myself with the disposing of marbles down the vents.

By December the belt-buckle overboard incident had seen the wear of two months passing, and, with the end of my first bag of marbles, I had felt my purge incomplete. So I had gone down to Amberson's and bought myself a new bag. These new marbles were of a less iridescent nature. Rather they were clouded—misty, and throughout the portion of the marble that lay inside the glass, ran hairy threads of milk white, vague and ghostly. It bothered me faintly to have to stuff such insecure-seeming marbles down the holes of the ventilator, but what had to be, had to be.

Miss Rama Stalk, Miss Kitty, and Mrs. Logg were seated in the parlor, religiously adhering to its radiator. This contraption, being in the parlor, was painted a rather dismal apple-green, and abloom with what I later discovered to be cherubs in the various stages of revelry, and semi-nude mermaids. The ladies assembled with the idea of gleaning a scant warmth from a furnace that only coughed up strange and horrible noises, accompanied by an occasional blast of cold air that it had scraped up from between the cracks of the icy cellar walls. In this season the walls had damp frozen onto them in paper-thin sheets of clammy and faintly green-hued ice.

My fingers let fall yet another marble. In the dim light of the foyer it shone a milky, beseeching blue. Its cry cut through the gray like a diamond.

A footstep sounded on the front porch. I could see, in the darkened upper corner by the door, the rope that had once been connected to a doorbell elevate itself several times. I called out, "Come in!"

Miss Tibbitt was a strange-looking lady even then.

She was anywhere from sixty on up, and possessed of pink hair and round, shiny turtle eyes that sank far back under her line of brow, and rolled with perpetual amazement as fish eyes roll in a jelly jar.

I dropped another marble down the radiator hole.

What was stranger than Miss Tibbitt was the rabbit she led on a leash.

I had seen rabbits before.

I had eaten chocolate ones on Easter.

I had watched them hotfooting it through our back yard in the fresh and violet morning before the wind had blown the dawn in.

But I had never seen one up close. And I had never seen

one on a leash. And I had never seen one that looked like Glorio.

I stood up and walked around the back of the registration desk.

The ladies, hearing the creak of floorboard as I jumped up, turned around and fixed Miss Tibbitt with a long community stare. It slowly reduced her to the consistency of powder. The stare then shifted to the rabbit, who was limping around in what appeared to be a circle, applying his quivering pink nose to certain portions of the rug.

"Goodness me!" exclaimed Miss Kitty, emerging momentarily from her stupor and pulling at her loose chin. "Is that creature going to mess on the carpet?" This said, Miss Kitty promptly fell back to sleep. Her chin receded into the groove that it had worn there throughout her ninety-four years.

Miss Tibbitt looked up quickly. "Oh no, ma'am," she said to the slumbering Miss Kitty, "my Glorio wouldn't do anything like that. He's just smelling the place out."

The rabbit looked up and met the stare of the ladies with a look sinister in its urbanity. He shook his hind foot in the air.

Miss Rama hit Miss Kitty with her elbow. "She says he's just smelling the place out."

"Well, Rama, how was I to know? Honestly!"

Miss Kitty fell asleep.

All the other ladies turned around, after giving rabbit and owner one more hard look. From the foyer I could feel their ears stretching out to us. Only one lady, Mrs. Logg, remained turned toward us. They picked up their fans.

I looked at Miss Tibbitt.

Miss Tibbitt looked at me.

Glorio looked at me.

I moved further behind the desk.

Glorio was, without a doubt, the most malevolent-looking creature that I had ever encountered.

Scrawny, in truth, a bag filled with various and ill-assorted bones, his body withdrew and then blossomed out in ways totally in dissent with the dictates of rabbit anatomy. From a few places upon this sack sprouted bristly hairs that could not have been called white even though nature had obviously intended them to be. They were a sort of yellow, a pale urine-like yellow. The hair was so thin as to become a transparency for the raw skin that lay beneath it, giving it a somewhat jaundiced blush.

Glorio was possessed of two rather world-weary ears, drooping in a most unrabbitly fashion. They were thin and transparent, membranes merely, covered again with only a grace of hair. The pounding blood vessels showed tubular and bulging against the fragile, almost nonexistent layer of skin.

Glorio had a nose that existed in an almost constant state of hypertension and, no doubt, a navel hidden somewhere between his numerous folds of belly skin. Glorio also had a game leg.

This leg he kept hoisted high in the air, a trick of rare strength and balance, so as not to infringe on his motion, which may be loosely termed hopping.

This leg Glorio utilized to its full capabilities—as an ultimate threat.

He could make a little swat with that leg, accompanied by a small song-and-dance routine executed by his beady eyes, which presented the victim with a good idea of his eventual fate should he cross the rabbit. This horrifying act Glorio performed right then. It was an action that stopped my heart in its flow and sent me creeping even further behind the desk.

Mrs. Logg sat disapprovingly in the parlor. "Well, miss," she said. Her hands were folded across her massive lap. Her eyes were like slits in her full, hard face. "What are you pussy-footing around for?"

I pointed to the rabbit.

"Is that a rabbit?" I asked.

Miss Tibbitt smiled uncertainly as if she too had entertained doubts. She looked on Glorio with eyes warm with love. "Sometimes people think it's maybe an aardvark. But aardvarks don't look like that. If people knew their business, they'd know it didn't look like an aardvark, not in the least."

"When I was a girl," said Miss Kitty, lighting on the word "aardvark." She rolled her head on her chest. "When I was a little girl, Mama had an aardvark shell. Uncle Ellenburg used it for a slop jar."

"No, dear," said Miss Rama Stalk. "That was an armadillo."

"It was?"

"Oh no, ma'am," I said. "I thought it was a rabbit, ma'am. I just wasn't sure."

Miss Tibbitt and I looked at each other.

"He likes to be kissed," said Miss Tibbitt. She looked uncomfortable. "It's only that he bites." She sighed and held up a hand sporting four fingers.

Glorio waved his hind leg in the air with remarkable dexterity.

I looked at Miss Tibbitt.

Miss Tibbitt looked at me.

I rubbed my toe against the splintery wood of the foyer floor in an effort to detach my toenail from its source.

"Can you tell me," said Miss Tibbitt at length, "where I can find a Mr. Carl Lamb?"

"Uncle Lamb? Uncle Lamb? He's my uncle. Uncle Lamb!"

I looked at Glorio.

Glorio looked at me.

"Oh, Uncle Lamb!" I called. I pointed to Glorio. "I've got to go," I said. "I've got to go and do . . . something. My uncle, he'll be here in . . ."

Glorio was advancing on my marble bag, which I had left by the vent.

"Oh, Uncle Lamb!"

"Yes! Yes! I'm coming!" shouted Uncle Lamb from deep inside the bowels of the commode. "I'm brushing my teeth!"

In a few minutes the sound of flushing spread loud and resonant from the bathroom. In these early days before Mrs. Turncew, Uncle Lamb always said he was brushing his teeth so as not to offend any of our sensitive ladies. In truth Uncle had no teeth—those visible were false. The originals had all been removed in that period when Floyd, the dentist by hobby, had ruled the house. He had promised to put them back—a service rendered impossible by his choice of method to evade the draft. Those things square and yellow and resembling teeth only in the remotest of ways, he kept some of the time in his mouth, and most of the time in a jar.

Uncle emerged from the commode and zipped up his pants. He patted his belly. He tucked back in a large piece of flesh that had stuck its head out of one of the holes of his T-shirt to peer at the world. He grinned at Miss Tibbitt. He saw Glorio. He crossed behind the desk to stand with me.

"Well, well, well," said Uncle.

He looked at Glorio.

"My name is Alice Tibbitt," said Miss Tibbitt.

"Is that an aardvark?" asked Uncle. He pointed to Glorio, who was still sneaking up on my marbles.

"Oh no," said Miss Tibbitt. She pulled at the fingers of her glove. "No, no, no, no—that's a little rabbit, a *bunny*."

The *bunny* eyed my marbles.

"I could have sworn it was an aardvark shell," muttered Miss Kitty. "Are you sure it wasn't an aardvark shell? Mary?"

I looked at my marbles where they lay, round and shiny and utterly vulnerable to attack. They crouched defenseless in the corner by the radiator. I considered the possibility of retrieving, thereby rescuing, them.

Glorio followed my eyes, and they lit once more upon the marbles, this time with a brighter light.

My heart contracted. I had betrayed them! My marbles! With horror I watched as Glorio limped over and sniffed at them, striking the bag with his nose until it fell over. The marbles came drifting out in a silky, blue procession and eyed Glorio with the cataract-clouded eye of innocence. Glorio sniffed at them. Then he ate one.

"My little bunny and I would like a room."

The little bunny threw up my marble.

"Yes, ma'am," said Uncle Lamb. "Would you step up and sign the register, please?"

Glorio sat, disgruntled, on his damp tail. He chewed his foot. He eyed the rejected marble with disgust. He kicked it.

"It certainly does *look* like an aardvark," said Uncle, lifting one eyebrow to look at Glorio. "You're sure he's not an aardvark?"

"Perhaps," suggested Miss Tibbitt helpfully, "his mother was an aardvark."

From the living room came the faintly hollow sound of Miss Rama thumping her chest. Miss Rama did not approve of interracial marriages.

"Emmeline," said Uncle Lamb, "take Miss Tibbitt's things up to eleven-b."

I looked at Glorio.

I shook my head.

"Go along now, Emmeline," said Uncle Lamb. I could feel the pressure of his finger at the small of my back. I took a step forward.

Glorio's ears, which had formerly been at half mast, straightened with remarkable electric force.

I took a step back.

Miss Alice Tibbitt smiled weakly at me. I wedged my way past Glorio, all the time adhering closely to the wall. I cast a mournful eye on that morsel of my childhood—the regurgitated marble—that had been so rudely used by this, a stranger.

Glorio sat. He waited.

I picked up the bags, of which there were two, and a covered birdcage.

"Careful! Careful how you handle that, child!" exclaimed Miss Tibbitt, pointing at the bag in my right hand. "You'll spill the innards all over the lining!"

I readjusted the bag on my arm.

Mrs. Logg piped up from the parlor, "What? What will spill?"

"Oh," Miss Tibbitt explained shyly. "The blood."

I put the bags down.

"It's rabbit blood. In cans. You see," she said, "it was one day about eight years ago, and I had just had an accident. I was in my sister's home in Canaan, up in Jefferson County, and she was running around the field trying to catch her husband Bowie's cow, and I said to her, 'You'll never catch that cow that way. You're only frightening him. Here, Butternut. Here, cow.' And she bit me. The cow. Well of course I bled and bled, and Sister didn't know what to do with me, bleeding out there in her husband Bowie's cow lot, and Butternut, that vicious animal, standing there with blood on her teeth, and I said, 'Sister, Sister, run, for heaven's sake, and get me some blood, because I am going to faint right here in the sun and freckle!'" Miss Tibbitt looked significantly around. "So Sister went and got Bowie's big truck, and we drove all over Jefferson County and into Tremble, and we found nary a bit of blood. I lay there in the car just panting and white to see —it was a wonder I lived. Sister had the cold fear in her heart. Right then I started thinking of disasters like that when blood is needed. My daddy," said Miss Tibbitt, "conducted the Katey Special. He had three wrecks. Whenever there'd be a wreck somewhere up the line, they'd wire it into Dennison —Dennison was the big train town in the Texas panhandle in those days—and Mama and me and Auntie Sweet would go down and wait for the news at the depot. Of course there was always a lot of blood, and someone was cutting their hand or whatnot." She breathed. "And then there are shipwrecks, boilers bursting. Once Sister and I, we went to a very private school in Dennison, Miss People's, and the boiler burst, and those oranges we kept in the basement—all over that building! It was terrible! Of course there was no blood, but there might have been. And altogether it come to me—I said, Alice Tibbitt, what would we do in the occurrence of a disaster when people went and ran out of blood?"

She paused to lend significance to her words.

"So I made the resolution right then and right there!" declared Miss Tibbitt. "I said, 'Alice, it's your responsibility, and nobody else's responsibility, to save blood in case it might be that there comes a disaster, and so I've saved every drop of blood I could. I have had eight little rabbits." She pointed to Glorio. "My Glorio is the ninth, and I have saved every little red drop of their blood. It lies, sir, in that one suitcase, sir and ladies." She pointed to the suitcase that I had held.

"Mark my words," said Miss Tibbitt, "we will need that blood someday." She looked at me.

"Yes, ma'am," I said.

"It makes sense," said Mrs. Logg, nodding her head.

Uncle dug the thickened sweat out from the wrinkles in his forehead. "Emmeline," he said. His large fingernail scraped into the bone of my spine. "Emmeline, the bags . . .''

I looked at him.

I looked at Glorio.

I picked up the bags. I crept over to the corner. With my one free hand, and my eye always upon the menace that was Glorio, I picked up my ill-used bag of marbles, scraping the glassy balls back into its mouth with a fast sweep of my hand. I stuffed it into the back pocket of my jeans.

Miss Tibbitt plucked the covered birdcage up off the floor and, swinging it with great abandon, followed me to the stairs. I stepped back and gave her the lead. We started up.

Our stairs were steep and quite narrow. They were the kind of stairs that, if you missed one step, the rest of your journey down would be accomplished on your rear end. They were closeted in by the thin veneer of plaster that Grandfather had bought and christened walls with. They reigned paramount throughout the entire house. They looked, and indeed were, of the consistency of paper, and painted, in the case of the hallway, an unfortunate sort of green. There were no windows in the hall, with the one exception of a triangular stained-glass affair fixed high up in the wall on its further end, which lent a tiffany-lamp red-and-lavender light that even further dehumanized the passage. All persons trespassing into its range were rendered a bilious and otherworldly green.

As Miss Tibbitt ventured up into this awful halo, Glorio remained perfectly immobile, resting sinisterly on his dismal clump of wet tail, eyeing me, eyeing my marbles. This lasted nearly thirty endless seconds.

Then time, in the form of the now-taut leash, compelled him to follow where it led, or relinquish neck and head to distant places.

Which is not to imply that Glorio actually *moved*. He merely changed his center of gravity, which resulted in his being pulled across the floor on his fanny, still fastening me with an eye that boded no good.

I mustered my courage and, elevating the bag, followed at a safe distance.

Miss Tibbitt had purple high heels on, snow-covered as the world they had so recently left at our doorstep, abloom at the toe with all manner of flora and fauna, most notably grapes, but also slightly flushed apples and an occasional tiny felt rose. Mounted one per toe were lady bugs, plastic constructions of an abstract sort, blazing red and ebony-black. They were possessed, collectively, of four rather half-hearted feelers, the tips lost among the folds of the minute roses.

The rabbit Glorio was being dragged unceremoniously behind her. His three good legs batted back and forth like gallery oars in an attempt to keep his stubby neck intact. The

[65

bad one was hoisted in the air and held with remarkable—nay, awe-inspiring—strength at what amounted to a right angle over his head.

I advanced cautiously, my eye ever on Glorio, bumping the precious suitcase against the narrow walls, barely missing Miss Kitty's prize-winning vase, composed of a Clorox bottle painted red and ornamented with felt flowers and tipsy celluloid bees emerging from its cut-off spout.

In turn, hastened and compelled though he may have been, Glorio was doing his level best to keep his eye on me. About mid-stair he turned around and fixed me with an ominous stare and ran into the steps with his chin. His evil, triangular face grew dark with hatred for me. His ears drooped until they dragged upon the floor.

Miss Tibbitt paused at the head of the stair.

Our house had lent itself admirably to the structure of a rooming house. The hall—the grotesque colors of its window stretching long and narrow, not unlike a neon finger, meeting Miss Tibbitt where she stood—was thin and dark, somehow damp, and alive with the many tall, flat-faced doors, eleven of them, hiding the rooms of our ladies.

Before each lay a bristling hair rug with the admonition "Welcome!" emblazoned on its hoary surface in letters of raised and discolored rubber. Eleven doors, and all were numbered, even Uncle's and mine. It was for appearance's sake.

I looked down the long expanse of hall. It seemed as if, at any moment, someone might come leaping out and scream, "Here's your ears!"

Miss Tibbitt knelt momentarily and patted Glorio on his knotted, serpent-like head. He swung around to take a bite at her. He missed. She straightened up. Her purple heels cutting into the carpet, she hurried down the hall, counting the numbers with her lips and completely missing 11-b, finally coming back to it.

Glorio leaped and puffed, trying to keep up with her. His

leash rode far up his narrow, stalklike neck. His cold eyes rolled malevolently in his head. His small and damp feet brushed rapidly across the floor.

Miss Tibbitt opened the door to 11-b.

The room had formerly belonged to Mrs. Pennial, that fragile ash of a woman who had drifted to her grave the season before. It was small, its dimensions just large enough to house a three-quarter's-width bed, a bureau, a washstand, a wardrobe, and a stuffed parrot.

This parrot was yet another remnant of my grandfather's taxidermic days upon this earth. It, even in its prime not the handsomest of fowls, was in this, what might be termed not its prime, the ugliest. It had swung avidly on its tin perch, which hung in the window at an odd angle, amounting to perhaps forty-five degrees, so that the parrot had slid very close to one end of the perch while ignoring the other completely. He had existed in this stance of favoritism for nigh onto forty years. The perch was fastened to the curtain rod by one old shoelace of mine.

Beneath the bizarrely acrobatic parrot sat the milk can Uncle had spray painted gold for Mrs. Pennial, and which she had made use of until the very day she dropped over dead. She had had a deep and abiding fear that she would lose her false hair down the commode in the black of the night.

The bed was a miracle of invention. It had been shipped from God knows where for God knows what reason to squat in this room like some Italian peasant. It was tall, rising from the floor a full two feet before encountering what could be termed the crosspiece. Out of sympathy to the parrot, with whom it had resided for so many years, and feeling itself akin, through nationality, to the leaning tower of Pisa, it sloped toward the inside of the room so sharply that the delicate Mrs. Pennial had found it difficult to stay on the bed.

This bed, in accord with its noble aspirations to become

America's leaning bedstead, had, within the framework of its construction, still another touch of that Italian old-world flavor: each bedpost was adorned with a magnificent Italian urn, with the exception of the northeastern one, which Grandfather, having run out of chickens to stuff, had sawed off and used as the base to a lampshade.

These urns were carved, wooden, such as one might find in a Genoan villa, and crawling with vines and tiny cherry-wood flowers. In the course of their crawling they managed to ooze and claim the greater portion of the headboard and the footboard, even shinnying down to touch with Mater Terra by dint of the legs.

Across from this spectacle of Renaissance debauchery crouched the bureau, which climbed from its claw feet to become a laudable facsimile of the Aswan figures. Housed between these two edifices of carving were a number of stained and ancient drawers. If you opened them, the smell of Mrs. Pennial came crawling out from their insides and swallowed the room. It was a smell of crushed and bruised violets in the first brown stages of rot.

Upon the bureau rested a dingy lavender lace doily, heavily reminiscent of the violet perfume with which Mrs. Pennial had anointed it at regular intervals, and one even dingier lavender pitcher and washbowl. This set, in addition to being the sole one of its kind to be purple, was beset with a variety of weeds set forth in alarming abundance and serving as the source of several big and frightfully hairy bees.

Fastened over this washbowl was a much-scratched and little-used mirror. Mrs. Pennial's late husband had been a railroad man, and had, like all railroad men, invested his money in diamonds. He kept his fortune on his women's fingers.

Growing suspicious in her later years, Mrs. Pennial took to scratching glass with the supposed diamonds that she wore on her narrow and bony fingers. Despite the fact that they always scratched, she was convinced that the diamonds were some ruse her husband had pulled on her. She scratched the window, and the glass eyes of the parrot, which, regarding this as an insult, promptly fell out.

The mirror was flanked by two cherubs holding light bulbs, and was topped by one stuffed halibut which Mrs. Pennial had said reminded her of her late husband.

The walls were papered. In somewhat overly handled array, the paper hung grudgingly on the walls. Which is not to say that the walls were completely papered—the papering came and went, rendering the wall abloom with alternate lavender sprays of violet, and bare spaces of ruffled plaster; for Mrs. Pennial had been the proud possessor of a yellow parakeet who, when hung in a certain spot, proceeded to eat the wallpaper off that certain spot.

The room, like the hall, was somehow damp; like the hall it was dark, being lit as it was by the scratched and frosted glass.

"Well," said Miss Tibbitt, putting the birdcage down, "it isn't the Orange Court."

While I was wondering what the Orange Court was, Miss Tibbitt swatted at the dust on the bed. It rose perhaps an inch into the air in indignation. It settled down to stare once more at the world in a thin, powdery white film. Miss Tibbitt swung the suitcase up onto the bed.

"Here, child," said Miss Tibbitt, opening the suitcase and taking out a can labeled Hawaiian Punch. I could see from where I stood other Hawaiian Punch cans, sandwiched carefully between cotton and old linens, all looking about the same. They were old now, and scratched. Their tops, where spouts had once been, were now covered tightly with black electrician's tape.

She handed me the can. "Be careful, now," she warned. "Don't spill it."

I looked at the can.

A sour, almost bittersweet smell hovered about it. I held it away from me.

"Ma'am," I said. "What do you want me to do with it?"

Miss Tibbitt looked up. Then she looked around the room. She put her finger in her mouth and, holding the fabric of the glove in her sparse teeth, began inching the glove off her skinny appendage. About mid-finger she muttered, "No icebox?"

"No, ma'am," I said.

Miss Tibbitt sat down on the bed, her finger still in her mouth. "No icebox?" she said. She tapped one of the cans absent-mindedly. She paused. She worked the glove down her fingers.

Glorio thumped his damp third leg up and down on the floor.

After a while I said, "Yes, ma'am, no icebox." I sat down on the bed next to her and sighed.

Glorio moved in closer.

I stood up.

After some five or ten minutes, Miss Tibbitt finished pulling her glove off. "Bathtub?" she asked. "Any bathtub?"

"Yes, ma'am," I said. "Yes, ma'am, there is. Over there." I pointed to the door joining her room to the bathroom and—I took a horrified look at Glorio—to my room on the other side of the bathroom.

Glorio favored me with a hungry look, and commenced to sidle up to me. I moved even closer to the door.

"Go fill it up with water an inch or two, and stand the cans in it. And quickly," said Miss Tibbitt. She smiled. "We don't want the blood congealing on us, now do we?"

I certainly did not want the blood congealing on me. I shook my head vehemently. The rabbit blood felt by its weight, and by its thick tendency to slide, like heavy tomato juice left out in the sun.

I edged toward the bathroom door.

"Oh, and little girl," she called. "Little girl, stand it *upright,* now do you hear, *upright!*"

I nodded again. I took another step forward.

Between me and the door sat Glorio, his limp and dry hair crusted and matted, his leg hoisted high over him in the act of applying his tongue to the nether regions of his body. At the small and tentative sound of my footfall, he froze. He remained, his head thrust under his leg, eyeing me. I stepped back.

"Oh," I said hastily, pointing to the label that proclaimed in dirty ball-point-pen ink on a small and torn piece of masking tape clinging to the rusty surface of the Hawaiian Punch can, the unlikely title of "Charlotte." "What does this mean, ma'am?"

Glorio lowered his leg sinisterly. He hit his nose.

"Oh," said Miss Tibbitt airily, "Charlotte was my fifth rabbit." She unpacked two more Hawaiian Punch cans bearing the proud names of "Eric" and "Haskell." She set them upright on the bed.

"Oh," I said.

I looked at Glorio.

I made a slow circle, keeping ever close to the wall, and with a darting action seized the cans "Eric" and "Haskell" and, with "Charlotte" already in tow, backed around Glorio. He pivoted his head three-quarters of the way around. Prying his clump of tail off the floor, he accommodated his neck the other quarter. He gave me the hairy eyeball.

Miss Tibbitt peeled off her other glove as if it were the outer layer of a butter bean, and threw it to Glorio. He caught it neatly.

I broke for the bathroom and, reaching the door in safety, flung myself inside.

Miss Tibbitt seized the end of Glorio's leash, so loosely draped about her wrist, and began to pull Glorio toward her, winding up the leash about her hand as she went. He continued sitting. When he had reached her ankles, she took the layered circle that she had formed, and placed it on the urnless bedpost.

Glorio stood up. He hoisted his leg heavenward and began to unwind himself, hopping around the bedpost. His eyes, except in that brief second when he turned, were fixed always on me.

I eyed Glorio.

Then I eyed the water heater. The water heater crouched in the corner of the bathroom, a shiny, silver demon. In hopes of attaining water, I turned its faucet.

The water heater rumbled.

It ruminated.

I hit the trunk of it.

It coughed up a small yellow stream of water, stopped, and stared insolently at me.

I hit it again.

This time the yellow stream widened and the thick, velvet water limped out to ooze along the bottom of the tub. I placed "Charlotte," "Eric," and "Haskell" gingerly in the rising liquid.

Glorio, a single loop standing between his teeth and my flesh, chortled into the glove.

I looked into the room.

In preparation for the kill, Glorio spit the glove out.

"Oh, Miss Tibbitt, ma'am," I said, "something has come up. Come down. I have to go that way." I pointed to my door. "I have to go to the bathroom." I started out.

Miss Tibbitt looked up brightly from her purple-and-red cans. "Make yourself at home, child," she chirped. With a wave of her hand she indicated the commode.

I sat down on it.

I looked at Glorio.

"Pull your pants down, child. It'll never do to do it that way," she said.

I pulled my pants down.

Miss Tibbitt deftly snatched the leash off the urnless bed-post and seized Glorio by his bad leg. She hung him out the window. "He needs airing sometimes," she explained. She thumped him vigorously against the outside wall. She returned to the bed and took out two more Hawaiian Punch cans, still holding Glorio by one wet foot. She passed me. I drew back against the tank of the commode. Glorio swung past me, eyeing me maliciously. One of his thin, waxy ears struck me. It felt disturbingly strong.

"Sam," she said. "And Lynn."

She turned off the water and flung Glorio carelessly into the bedroom.

I stood up quickly and pulled up my pants. "Well," I said heartily, edging toward the door that connected the bathroom with my bedroom. "Gotta go. Good-bye." I made a flying leap at the door handle and swung the door shut behind me. Then I locked it.

CHAPTER *Eleven*

It was March.

Mornings came, and my body seemed to me to become a silent and unruly cavern. Inside of me I could hear the distant, ever so inner rumblings of my secret barges loaded with the burnt remains of Mrs. Turncew's calcified repasts.

I woke early that month, propelled by some unknown cause to seek each dawn for myself. Hurrying down the stairs—my bare, thick-soled feet clinging momentarily on the steps rendered gooey by Mrs. Turncew's obsession with the marriage of wood and linseed oil—I watched the world before a dawn wind blew in to wash from it its other-world color. Wasted, chill, it was a land in interim, a link between the death of night and the darker sphere of daylight. I saw it alone, sheathed in one of Uncle's old T-shirts, my feet, ripple-fleshed with the cold, pulled under me, the tip of my bare bottom resting warily on the icy step. From somewhere deep in the tall grass I could see a frog's eyes, bright and inhuman, slide open and shut, from out of the marsh and the cold water sharp with crystals of ice, deep, fishless in this dawn. And far to the west a windmill scraped and caught on the sky.

March had come in like a lion and, due to the lion's greater size and ferocity, had devoured the lamb where it hid, and proceeded to rule even these, the last days of that month.

The river down the bluff was breaking in great surges of crested ice brown as the water it was formed from. It moved to pile under the fragile and lacy Candlemar Section Bridge in a dangerous backup that began to send the icy chocolate waters sliding insidiously into the shallow fields next to the highway, and in spreading fingers across the road. A warning of spring floods.

But it was not yet spring. The town still lay silent under the threat of winter, except for the occasional groan of a tree shifting its weight of snow to some other shoulders, silent and smooth, and slowly sinking into the earth.

It was in mid-March that Uncle—while practicing elocution in the bathroom in the manner of Demosthenes—swallowed four rather large stones, not in the manner of Demosthenes. He came staggering out of the bathroom, with his hands clapped tight about his throat to prevent a fifth pebble from making the journey that its fellows had just undertaken. Refusing to return to his mouth, it insistently pushed downward.

Uncle, clutching his throat, stumbled around the room madly, his tongue flopping from his mouth, his face turning a slow red.

I put down my marble bag on the floor of the foyer and looked at him quizzically.

Mrs. Turncew sprang up from the parlor floor where she had been tending to the African violets in the coffin—they stubbornly died every time their fragile roots were lowered into soil—and threw her trowel across the room, hitting a chicken lamp on the head. The chicken lamp spun frantically around until it collided with the fan from the Groce Funeral Home and fell rattling onto the floor.

I stuck a marble in my mouth and rolled it around.

Uncle fell into the banister and sank to the floor, still clutching his throat. I could see the outline of the pebble where it was.

"Lamb! Lamb!" screeched Mrs. Turncew. She ran over to the banister and, lowering one limb, then picking it up to

[75

lower another one, finally deposited both on the ground, and carefully tucked her blossoming dress under her. "What is the matter? Oh Lamb!"

Uncle Lamb rolled his eyes about wildly.

"Oh, Emmeline!" whispered Mrs. Turncew, turning to me. Her face was ashen. "It's his heart."

Uncle kicked his feet and threw his head back and forth.

"Lucinda! Lucinda! Help! It's Mr. Lamb!"

Lucinda scurried in. She stood there and heaved.

I stood up and put my hands in my back pockets. I walked around in front of Uncle Lamb and looked at him.

"Get some towels, Lucinda! We must keep him warm!"

Lucinda's eye was suddenly shot through with light. She stopped heaving and charged for the linen closet.

I kicked the corner of the rug with my big toe.

"Oh, Lamb, Lamb!" cried Mrs. Turncew in despair. A large yellow tear rolled down her face. "My darling Lamb!" Impulsively, she seized his head to her breast. Uncle swallowed the stone.

He sat there by the banister for a minute. A peculiar light came into his eye. He stood, pushing Mrs. Turncew away from him, and looked down at his stomach. He felt it experimentally.

I looked in through the parlor at the linen closet, where Lucinda was hurriedly pulling out towels, sticking one inside her dress bosom, one beside her to carry in to Uncle, another into her dress bosom, and so on.

Uncle pulled out his stomach and then let it recede. He walked around the room.

Mrs. Turncew sat on the floor, staring at him.

"Lamb," she began.

"It's all right, Lucinda!" I called. "He's all right!"

Lucinda looked up at me quickly and then, enfolding her bulging bosom with her massive arms, hotfooted it off to the kitchen.

Uncle punched his stomach. He lifted it up. He dropped it down. He swayed to swing it before him.

"I've got to go," mumbled Uncle Lamb, looking at his stomach. "I've got to go to the hospital." He looked at the hatrack and pulled his homburg off of it. He put it on.

"But Lamb!" cried Mrs. Turncew, trying to scramble to her feet.

Uncle waved her aside and opened the front door slowly. Delicately he closed it behind him. He wandered off down the street, gazing unhappily at his huge, swinging stomach.

Mrs. Turncew came to the window and stood there, watching him go. Since she was taller than I, I could feel her warm, bittersweet breath pour down on my head.

CHAPTER *Twelve*

Uncle stayed in the hospital for five days.

On the first day they pumped his stomach out.

On the succeeding days they tried to make him vacate his bed.

On the fourth day Mrs. Turncew, who had been forbidden to see him, was allowed in as the hospital's ultimate weapon. Mrs. Turncew brought with her a plate of greenies.

Greenies were concoctions of sugar and a great deal of butter, green by dint of food dye. They were alive with raisins rendered green by the diabolical methods of science, and stiffened by corn starch to give them shape. Standing balls of icing, they had an incredible sweetness that, when taken into the body, swelled to fill the entire inside of you with sugar, growing to possess your head, your stomach. The sweetness filled the air about them, pungent, deadlier than liver, more ominous than onion.

It was to these bloated blobs of sugar that Uncle was exposed so soon after his pebble-swallowing ordeal—a veritable array of them—in all shapes, in all sizes, in all shades of green. There were forest-green greenies, and mint-green greenies, and pea-green greenies, and sea-green greenies. Mostly there were bilious greenies. One by one, greenie by greenie, Mrs. Turncew forced them down Uncle's protesting throat.

That evening Uncle had his stomach pumped out again.

During the process, in the waiting room Mrs. Turncew confided to the orderly that she felt it would be best if Mr. Lamb returned home following this second pumping out, so as to re-cover where loving hands hovered. The orderly immediately acquiesced.

Before Uncle was fully aware of what was going on, he was bodily shipped out of the hospital, carried down the wintry streets of Chaucy, hauled past the coffin in the parlor and up the stairs to his old room. Mrs. Turncew kept him trapped there for five days. At the end of that time, Uncle, on pretense of having to brush his teeth, escaped once more to the down-stairs bathroom. Later that day he shoved a piece of paper under the door, with an order to buy a security lock for the bathroom door, and a small wedge of dollar bills folded into it. Mrs. Turncew read the note, put it in her apron pocket, and hid the money away in an empty Collarium bottle.

CHAPTER *Thirteen*

In mid-March came also to the silent streets of Chaucy the call of Mrs. Larbuck, who, for some reason, had taken a notion that I was trying to steal the cherries from her tree.

Mrs. Larbuck had but two evidences of greenery—a rather half-hearted boxwood, and a small and spindle-branched cherry tree that was her pride, her treasure, her all-consuming concern—except in the three months of summer.

When summer came and the cherries unfolded from their blossoms, I would crawl on my belly through the high grass of her back yard and snatch at them from my hiding place.

They were wonderful cherries, round and with a fibrous, rosy outer layer and a soft, sour, sweet pulp within. I would steal them, then steal them again. Mrs. Larbuck walked her roof all summer. She did not once notice me.

Only in the winter did she appear. Sun disappeared, gone into hiding so many worlds away from our world. The town shut itself tight behind the door of snow, and Mrs. Larbuck would stand on top of her silver roof, snow-covered in places. She was clad only in a lavender body wrapper and red woolen scuffs, which, scraping against the tin, could be heard all over the block. The only protection she provided for her bullet head was the dubious one of some forty-odd crimper curlers.

"I know you're there, Emmeline Lamb! Emmeline Lamb! I know you're in there! You stop stealing my cherries!"

In the silent town you could hear her voice, wavy and sad as a foghorn. It broke the vibrations of the snow. It cut deep into the water-sleep of life.

"I know you're there, Em Lamb!"

And silent and solitary the narrow cherry tree stood, bare and sheathed in ice in this last moment of winter.

March was remarkable in that it was the month when Verbena first began her mysterious assault upon the flora of our community.

Verbena Fosbrink occupied the house on the corner of Lee Ambrose and Milk. In my younger days I remember a girl, thin-shouldered and narrow-breasted, with a body that blossomed in a huge, elephantine swell of thigh and calf. She looked like a strong tree deprived of all its leafery, sharpened to the point of her knobby head. Shadowed by the eaves of the small Victorian porch that rose straight and rectangular from the ground like some overly decorated pillbox hat, she seemed very gentle, otherworldly, silent, and soft, with the unbelievable transparency of a hummingbird. I remember her dressed in a loose lavender housecoat that caught only momentarily on her small crest of bosom, and then fell to cling at her calf. She was seated far to the left to avoid the wide shaft of yellow sunlight driving through a jagged hole in the roof that Mrs. Phrygia Fosbrink had made one day while trying to take a sun bath on the steep and smooth-with-age tiles. Mrs. Fosbrink had slid inadvertently to a point of roof not sufficiently strong to bear up her some-two-hundred pounds; result coming in the wake of provocation, the beams had snapped.

I watched her catch with her pale hands at the flight of butterflies. Her hair drifted and surrounded her face in a thousand frenzied gold-and-white curves. Her eyes seemed almost lashless. When the lids slid over her pale, globular eyes, only a barely visible line of tiny reddish hairs was visible, and her lips had no color. They seemed mere stopping places in her face, never completely shut; from the inside of her came a soft sucking sound.

She would gather her knees to her narrow chest; with her lips just a little open, she would stare at the wretched sun as it burned out its aura. Once she had given me some old jewelry: a bracelet made of tiny powder-blue flowers with white rhinestone centers, a tin covered wagon off an old dime-store charm wrist-ring.

She was also albino.

Up to March of that year, Verbena had remained silent. She was content to rest in the shadowed cool of her house, or in the leaning, gray old porch. But in mid-March Verbena got the spirit: she began to take action.

Verbena was a carnivore. She ate only meat. She would never touch tooth to branch, to weed, to asparagus or aspidistra.

About the time when Uncle had just suffered through his second attack of the stomach pump, Verbena Fosbrink began a remarkable campaign to free, for all time, all the shrubbery from the soil that bound it. She changed in a day from the quiet, gentle girl I had once sat with in silence on windless days. From her shade world she emerged, clothed—so as to escape the rage of the blistering sun on her heat-sensitive skin— from toe to ear, and from her feet to the top of her head. Her eyes, which I had always imagined to be a shade approximating Glorio's sinister pink, were wedged behind a pair of heavy Jane-Russell-wears-them sunglasses. She wore a red knitted cap, coming down low over her eyebrows. It covered her entire head; only the bottoms of her ashen ears were left long and loose and flapping in the wind, occasionally graced by puffs of dirty white hair which floated out of her, under the cap, at a steady clip. Verbena was going bald.

I don't know the cause of this. Perhaps it was due to distress over her unfortunate lack of pigment. Perhaps it was heredity —her family evidenced a general lack of skull coverage. The gallery of thin-faced, hairless (and this description included women as well as men) daguerreotypes, hanging like death masks on the small, and fortunately dark, walls of the Fosbrinks' dining room, indicated this. They seemed not unlike presences from the other, more shadow-ruled world, admonitions to their hairy young of their eventual fate.

Then again, and this was Mrs. Logg's opinion, Verbena's paucity of hair could possibly be attributed to rebellion against the sordid way in which she had been raised.

Ruie Fosbrink, her father, was the Greyhound bus driver— the only Greyhound bus driver, therefore the only bus driver, in and about Chaucy. His route encompassed twenty-eight miles—fourteen miles to Urba, where a good many Chaucites were employed at the Eli Lilly pill factory, and fourteen miles back to Chaucy again.

The Greyhound bus people were hot for business: Ruie would wing back and forth, from Chaucy to Urba, ten and sometimes twelve times a day. As quitting time drew nigh, he would knock off in whichever town he happened to be near.

This was all very well and good in his youth; but when Ruie reached thirty-one, he decided that it was nigh about time he settled down. He married the former Phrygia Paully and, that lady proceeding to blow up like a huge pink elephant balloon, had the daughter, Verbena.

Ruie decided that he liked married life so well that he married another lady, a cousin of mine, Altherea Lamb, in Urba, and had seven children by her.

Ruie was a fair man. On the day he married Cousin Altherea, he decided that he would divide his nights equally between his two wives, his two families. He alternated, spending one night in Chaucy, the next in Urba. This seemed laudable to me. It was only after Mrs. Logg declared it to be like unto the Old Testament, therefore evil, that I saw the true light.

Whatever the reason, Verbena was going bald, and going bald with rare enthusiasm. Unattached hair followed her, outlining her shadow in the dusk in a white, soft fineness.

CHAPTER *Fourteen*

I went out on the back porch to watch Lucinda make the soap.

Lucinda was tucking one of Miss Tibbitt's good lace doilies into her trunk, which she kept in her compartment off the back porch. The door was open. In the dim shadows I could see Lucinda as she knelt on the floor beside the old steamer trunk.

"Lucinda," I called.

She looked up and then smiled at me. Lucinda didn't mind. Everybody knew she stole the linens. Once every three weeks or so Uncle would give her some pocket money and tell her to go and catch the movie at the Criterion in Mt. Vernon, and he would clean out her trunk and distribute the linens to the various sources from where they had sprung. The next day Lucinda would start patiently in again. But the pile of linens seemed larger. Uncle had not been out of the bathroom for two weeks solid now.

Big as she was, Lucinda was immaculate. Her whole body oozed cleanliness. Her clothes smelled vividly clean. The scent of them, fresh and stiff, hit you whenever you came within sniffing distance of her.

Lucinda had a shower in her compartment, with a torn, ragged curtain that observed "Jesus saves," and a small drainage. Every day, twice a day, Lucinda would stand fully clothed in her three-item wardrobe and give herself a good scrubbing down.

Then she would take off the coat and give her blouse and skirt a good scrubbing. Then she shed the remainder of her clothes and scrubbed her naked body three times. She would drench herself in camphor and rinse herself once more.

She would then sit down on the cement floor of the shower, an action which took some doing and about five minutes' time altogether. She let down one limb, raised it to accommodate another's lowering, then gathered them together as she turned on the faucets, and finally spread them out as she reached with her old wizened hand and seized her foot.

Painstakingly she spread out her toes; minutely she cleaned them, thrusting her huge, square nails between them to dig out whatever indomitable dirt had managed to force its way down there during the twelve hours of cease-fire, and through the heavy hide of weighty nursing shoes.

She did not wear the shoes in the shower. They were kept clean by the use of two red woolly socks, and a daily polishing with a washcloth.

With more time than she had spent lowering herself to the floor, she would pry herself off the floor and trot naked to the mirror, in front of which she vigorously cleaned those teeth remaining to her with a strong and bristling brush.

Lucinda's wrapper was the only other item of clothing she possessed that any of us knew about. It was pink; the remnants of nylon lace hung raggedly to the curve of the collar, to the tiny pockets which shielded each nipple of Lucinda, and to the puffed sleeves that caroused halfway down Lucinda's arm. With this wrapper laid across her body, she would run down to the demon furnace to hang her clothes against its great white belly. Sometimes they dried. Sometimes they didn't. When they didn't, Lucinda wore them anyway.

Lucinda spoke with great care. All of her words were sprung from her mouth. She had worked for years on it with Uncle Lamb, who had sat on the chicken coop in the long days of the shifting seasons, watching her as she made lye soap, and calling out the words to her, which she then called back.

She looked up at me and said, "Hello, Emmie."

"What is that?" I asked. I pointed to the doily she held in her hand. "One of those bureau things?"

"Sure is," said Lucinda proudly, holding it to the scant light. "Real pretty, ain't it not?"

"Sure is," I said. I walked off the porch and out into the back yard.

"Lucinda! *Lucinda!*" called Miss Tibbitt from the upstairs window. "Come up here and string my rosary beads!" She stuck her old head out the window. "You hear! Stop that scratching and get your hide into this house!"

Lucinda deposited her doily in the trunk and crossed the back yard to the lye pot. She scratched her arm.

"I am not *prone* to string beads for no Catholic," said Lucinda loudly, well knowing that Miss Tibbitt only called her pearls her rosary, and attended the First Congregational Church each Sunday and Wednesday. Lucinda rolled up her sleeves carefully and clawed at a large scab on her arm. She rolled her sleeve down and began to stir the pot with a long paddle that Uncle had stolen once from a canoe in Lake Goshorn. "Three little fishes and a mama fishy *too*," she sang in her low, rumbling voice.

I caught the porch rail and swung around on it.

The stuffed parrot from Miss Tibbitt's room fell out of the window and hit me on the head.

"*Lucinda!*" bawled Miss Tibbitt. "How many times have I told you to get into this house and string my rosary beads! I am," she added sulkily, "in need of prayer. Now where did that parrot go?"

The parrot had landed in the ivy at my feet. I picked him up. His leg came off in my hand.

Lucinda stirred the soap. The pot was a heavy, huge black

8 6]

one, borne up by four heavy sticks, in reality the trunks of young trees, spread out from each other at the bottom and meeting. It was a jointure encouraged by a heavy rope looped around all four. Beneath the pot an orange fire burned, and the air around it was filmy and water-like.

"*Lucinda!*" With a violent flop, Miss Tibbitt swung Glorio out of her window and, holding him by one slender leg, whammed him against the side of the house. Small clouds of dust blossomed up from him.

I moved lest she should drop him on me.

Lucinda turned and, placing her hard, cracked hands on her massive hips, waddled halfway across the lawn. "And *whom*," she said witheringly, "do you think you're talking to, anyways?" She turned on her heel and, swinging her hips coyly, waltzed back to the cauldron and nattily began "Don't Sit under the Apple Tree with Anyone Else but Me."

The slow, creaking shudder of Mrs. Logg's window being raised scraped behind us.

Lucinda stood up ramrod straight.

Lucinda was unafraid of death, of cowboys, of giant ants, or the hound of the Baskervilles. She was afraid of Mrs. Logg.

Mrs. Logg's buffalo head rolled out of the window on the first floor. She laid her heavy arm on the sill with a loud thump. Silence.

"Lucinda," said Mrs. Logg. "Stop that scratching and get into this house."

Lucinda, who had not been scratching for a full ten minutes, scratched vehemently. "Miz Loagg," she said, sinking back into her Dennison diction, "Miz Loagg, Ah got de lye on de fire. Wif h'its boilin'. Ah can leave Miz Emmie out chere wif de lye gone boilin'. Bof dat an' she playin' wif de gun!"

As if on cue I went over and picked up Uncle's BB gun and dove into the window of the chicken coop to fetch out a Falstaff beer can.

Mrs. Logg threw her cat out the window. "You send Miss Emmie in here. She hasn't got any business playing with that gun." She closed her window.

The cat, whose name was Orson, stretched his long, lean body out until all the ribs drew apart. Then he compressed and, neatly, fitted them back together again. Orson dove into the ivy and started to methodically leap about. Orson had fantasies. He saw birds.

I dug up three Falstaff beer cans and set them up on the fence. I aimed my gun.

With a savage war cry, Orson sprang on something in the bush. He came up with an ivy leaf in his mouth. He slipped in and out of the ivy and ran toward me, prancing with his victim.

I shot one beer can. I shot two. It wasn't any fun. I was eight, and the greatest joy in the world, the most wonderful thing imaginable, the most stimulating experience possible was seeing Tarzan, tied to four elephants, one appendage to each beast: at the bidding of a slant-eyed general-white-slaver-desperado, they would part ways, an action which was designed by the villain to part Tarzan.

How disappointing when the elephants responded to some gentle word from Tarzan in elephant language! Or when Flash Gordon thwarted Emperor Ming's giant lizard. Or when Tarzan found an escape route out of the burial tower being slowly blocked up by the evil high priestess. Or when Flash Gordon found the trap door in the alligator pit just when the net was going to break and plunge him to his doom. Then there was the Blob—they always killed the Blob just before he got around to engulfing the hero's demented bobby-soxer of a girlfriend. Flash Gordon, John Carter of Mars, Tarzan, the Blob . . . I lived in frustration.

There was no sport in shooting cans. They didn't bleed. They only dribbled a little.

I put the BB gun down against the chicken coop and wiped my nose.

The remaining can shone in the late March sunlight that spun out of the phantom crystal cradled in the sky. It was that afternoon that I first saw Verbena at work.

Far in the growing sharpness of twilight, I could hear a loose, wet, flapping sound which came furtively to my ears from behind the chicken coop. I stopped scratching my nose and listened for a minute. With my hands I pulled myself up on top of the coop, and remained suspended for what seemed an interminable amount of time, with my belly forced against the ridge, before I was able to hoist my body up over it.

Up in the March sky a bird, bright with a panel of purple, a stripe of green, wheeled in flight. There existed the chill smell of moisture in every air cell. The world, except for the renegade grass bending slightly under an invisible wind that sent the blades curling about each other, fell silent. It waited.

Verbena peered around the corner of the Larbuck's garage.

I squashed myself close to the roof and scratched my nose.

Verbena scanned the area. She emerged, stooped, almost to a kneeling position. Then she did kneel. Her knees caught on the ground. It was clear in this moment before the night, and I could see her distinctly, with her big, flapping feet encased in heavy, hairy socks. Verbena wore corded trousers, which swelled and almost split at her huge, long thighs, and a duck-hunting jacket. She was in full head regalia—she wore the sunglasses, the cap. In the light I could see her ears clearly: they were alive, swollen, very pink with the cold. Their long tips caught under the cap, folding almost in two. With an impatient gesture Verbena pried them out and mashed them back into shape. There was a trowel in her hand. She looked banefully up at the roof where, of winter months, Mrs. Larbuck walked.

[89

"And as for your geraniums!" The hoarse, disembodied voice of Mrs. Larbuck rang out from one of the darkened attic windows. A gaunt hand reached out, encircled a meat-red pot of plastic-covered geraniums, and flung it over the edge.

Verbena froze.

"Why, YOU!!"

The sound of muted cursing, of scraping and struggle sounded. Mrs. Larbuck screamed shrilly, "That's my hair!"

A few seconds later a crimper curler, not totally without hair, came drifting down.

The Larbucks were a little testy. It was the rain and the hail all the time beating on the tin roof.

Verbena remained in her frozen state for a number of minutes. Then her eyes rolled a little. I could see the dim ghost of their life moving warily behind the sunglasses. Slowly she came to life. A hand that moved. A foot. Behind the yellow-gray of the sunglasses came a positive glare.

Dropping to one knee, then the other, she began to steal through the grass, stopping at regular intervals to cock her ear in the direction of the window.

The crimper curlers, one by one, came floating out of the window.

Orson leapt on something to the rear of me, and uttering a sanguinary, unearthly scream, tore into it. I turned my head just slightly. It was a palm fan one of the ladies had dropped.

Verbena reached the boxwood. She hesitated before it, caressing it with her unseen eyes. She dug savagely into turf, reaching down into the bone of earth and scraping soil out from its many small wormlike roots. I heard her murmur something. I strained my ears to hear it. She repeated it, this time more loudly.

"Slavery," whispered Verbena between clenched teeth.

I leaned over the edge of the chicken coop and watched her. My mouth dropped open and, as the digging progressed and Verbena grew more vehement in the boxwood's unearthing, it slid open until, had I not had a lower jaw, the upper might have fallen into the tall grass that heralded the Larbuck boundary and the back of the chicken coop.

Verbena threw down the trowel. Breathing fast and hard, she seized the tree by its narrow trunk and wrested it from the ground.

I shut my mouth. There were birds around.

Suddenly Verbena leapt to her feet and, twisting about to face the house, held the boxwood by its roots. *"Free!"* she cried. *"Free!"*

The boxwood, top-heavy as boxwoods tend to be, veered dangerously to the right.

I nearly fell off the chicken coop.

"Free! Free! Bush, you are FREE!!*"*

The boxwood, straining to maintain an upright position, desperately ignored Verbena.

I swung my leg onto the slightly slanted roof of the chicken coop in an effort to stay on. My toes elongated and dug into the slick tiles.

Verbena turned around and eyed the bush. She brushed the soil off her trousers with her free hand. She cocked her head.

Crimper curlers drifted delicately out of the window.

Verbena scratched her nose. She reached behind her glasses and scratched her eyeball. "Uh," she said hesitantly. "You're free."

The bush took a sharp dive to the left.

Verbena paused and scratched her eyeball again.

Desperately I arched my back in an attempt to re-establish myself on the roof. At the bottom lurked broken glass, choice pieces of jagged pottery, and a number of Uncle's beer cans that were the outdoor type.

"Uh, you'd . . . you'd like me to . . . to sort of . . . put you down?" Verbena asked helpfully. She eyed the dipping and looping bush with alarm. "You'd like for me to kind of . . . lay you down?"

The bush dove to the left.

I hammered my legs tight against the roof and drew my body up on the roof again.

Verbena looked at the bush. She dropped it.

She tapped her foot.

She took a piece of toilet paper out of her pocket and blew her nose on it.

She looked at the bush again.

The bush wallowed in the dirt for a few seconds and then lay quiet.

Verbena knelt down and picked up the trowel. She walked out of the yard and down the street.

Verbena's was a thankless crusade.

I could hear Lucinda's heavy footsteps once more crossing the yard. She shifted her great weight about the lye pot. The long paddle made harsh, sucking sounds as it drew away from the tenacious, thick liquid.

In the utmost secrecy Verbena plotted out her attacks. With careful deliberation she thought of any possible deterrent force; she took into consideration every detail, the degree of unwillingness of the root to part with its warden of earth, the timidity of the flora to seek liberty, the determination of the slave owner to keep the slave in bondage.

It was with great stealth that, through the back yards of the oppressors, she crept. It was with speed and skill that she extracted from their cold and earthy prison the shrubbery of our neighborhood.

Yet they lay there. The shrubbery just lay there. Verbena had freed nearly a hundred small trees and bushes. With the sweat of her brow, she had washed their roots with the sweet water of their freedom. And they lay there. In the sun, and in the slow whisper of late winter's rain, they alternately dried and sunk into damp, meditative rot, rooted with the woody wet, a hundred of them.

It was to this—this infamous, inglorious death—that these were reduced. Apathy. Apathy. That was all there was.

Verbena, like all true revolutionists, preceded her revolution. But the knowledge was in her. The responsibility lay in her hands. Verbena Fosbrink must lead the way, must wrest the path through the wilderness of unfeeling, unknowing, uncaring. She must illuminate a road that ten billion of the globe's plants would follow; she must strike the spark in the heart of the flora of the world . . . perhaps of the universe. Verbena could see them, rising, rising, marching behind her as one never-ending, always-stretching shadow. It was to this end that God had shaped Verbena.

Her figure fell away behind a line of trees in the distance.

I fell off the chicken coop.

In the twilight Orson screamed a victory scream over his prey. I watched the last crimper curler fall like a floating, spiraling butterfly—a fragile shadow in this, the brown light that preceded the darkness of night. Up in the crystal sky, a moon silently slipped into place and opened wide its flower.

CHAPTER *Fifteen*

Throughout March Uncle refused to speak to Mrs. Turncew through the heavy wooden door of the bathroom. She would pound on the door, pressing her whole figure close against it, fitting into the panels.

Eventually she took to sneaking around the side of the house and, her eyes shielded by one hand and her head turned away from the window, would clamber through the bare space of has-been flower beds and scratch against the windowpane.

One day Uncle emerged, went to the phone—his hand hovering about his zipper, threatening, on any sudden move of hers, to pull it down—and called Amberson's. He ordered curtains made and hung in the bathroom window. They were a riot of daisies and hibiscuses, swimming up from the bottom of the sill, an action which constituted what Amberson's thought of as a border, to stare at a vast expanse of white cotton above. With an eye on Mrs. Turncew he also ordered the security lock that she hadn't, big and black and lacy with etching, fitted with two keys.

CHAPTER Sixteen

"Sit still, Mary," said Mrs. Logg, reaching into her dress bosom with one twisted white finger and pulling her brassiere away from her gummy skin. "This is very important."

Uncle Lamb came sneaking through the living room. He was wearing his old and holeyest T-shirt. Cautiously he scratched the stubble that was darkening his chin. He looked around. "Where is she?" he whispered.

"In there," I whispered back, pointing to the kitchen.

"Mary! Don't whisper!" Mrs. Logg hit me squarely on the head with her thimble.

"Oooohhhh," said Uncle. He peered into the kitchen. He rubbed his chin once more. "Ooooh." He shifted up his pants and snuck off in the opposite direction. Immediately there ensued a violent squeaking of floorboards. In varying tones, all of them conflicting and quite loud, they began whining and uttering high-pitched squeals of alarm. Uncle turned around, trying in vain to silence them. Realizing his danger—heralded by the sudden gulf of silence from the kitchen, and then a frantic dropping of several cast-iron pans and a hasty slapping of what sounded like watery batter into a tin pan—he made a dash for the bathroom. He caught the door just in time.

Mrs. Turncew came charging into the parlor, brandishing a pan of lilac batter.

Lilac batter was spread on trays in little round lumps after it had been refrigerated an hour or so, whereupon, when thrust into an oven, it blossomed into little round lumps, the only difference being that they were now harder. They were invariably a sort of magenta hue.

But right then, in their more liquid form—I say "more" because in their finished state they are less liquid—they swam about, large dollops of water sliding coyly about the surface of the sluggish purple mass.

"Lamb! *Lamb!*" she called. She turned to us. "I thought I heard Lamb."

"You did," said Mrs. Logg. "He's in . . ." Mrs. Logg paused delicately.

Mrs. Turncew looked dejectedly at the door. "I wanted to bring him some lilacs," she said. "Men always do like batter."

I looked at the batter.

The batter leered at me. It sent its pearls of water sliding like giant amoebae drunkenly along the surface of the lilacs.

Mrs. Turncew took one more look at the bathroom door, turned, and walked thoughtfully off.

From the commode came the sound of two hard flushes, then another softer, more hesitant one. It faded.

Mrs. Logg whacked me again on the head with her thimble. "Mary, turn around and listen to this. It's good for you."

I turned my head.

She reached out and drew the stool where I was sitting deeper between her massive legs. She kicked me for good measure. "Ah hum," said Mrs. Logg. "The Bible. By Jesus Christ."

In the dim light she opened a large black book with a narrow gold cross emblazoned on the front. Outside, through the gauze of curtain, I saw something green and fat fall.

"Oh! That *parrot!*" came Miss Tibbitt's voice from up the stairs.

"Genesis," said Mrs. Logg. "Chapter One. 'In the beginning God created the heaven and the earth. And the earth was without form, and void, and darkness was upon the face of the deep. And the Spirit of God moved upon the face of the waters.' "

Something caught my attention.

"What?" I said. "Read that again."

Mrs. Logg smiled. She patted my head. " '. . . and the Spirit of God moved upon the face of the waters.' "

I saw an ocean. It was still. And in the gray throes of dawn it seemed endless. Still on the surface and at the same time . . . oddly turbulent: it was as if beneath its glazed and smooth face all the demons and daemons of a universe lay, churning the black water with their black hands. With a silent and a mighty roar, a bare, sweeping wind blew up across the motionless infinity of sea. . . . A great foot in a frog flipper came down and broke the surface of the water.

"Go on," I said.

Mrs. Logg read the first chapter, the second chapter, the third and the fourth. I liked them. I really liked them. I especially liked Jacob and Esau. Jacob had it all figured out, slick and perfect. He was as good as the Thin Man.

I began to look up to Mrs. Logg with a great deal more respect than I formerly had. She really did read some good things. The last thing she had made me read was an Elsie Dinsmore book. I hated Elsie Dinsmore. Mrs. Logg said that I must read it and discover in Elsie what I, Mary (Emmeline), would be like if I were a good little girl.

In the book, Elsie's father asked Elsie to play a Mozart piece on the piano for a guest, but, as it was Sunday, Little Elsie Dinsmore would only play hymns. She sat on the piano stool and held her breath until she turned blue and fainted.

Elsie Dinsmore seemed to me a thoroughly disagreeable child. I set a milk glass on the book's cover one whole night and neatly obliterated her smirking visage, which adorned it. I pulled out *Tom Swift and His Motorcycle* and read that, then *Gary Grayson's Football Rivals,* then *In the Land of Volcanoes.*

Orson pounced on the parrot in the bushes, screaming a cry of ecstasy.

Miss Kitty and Miss Tibbitt came down the stairs arm in arm. Miss Tibbitt was wearing a navy-blue dress with white daisies strewn over it in a highly eccentric pattern. Her narrow hands were covered by gloves. With one hand she tried to keep Miss Kitty's head from implanting itself too firmly upon her shoulder, where she was apt to fall asleep.

"Oh, Mary!" she said to Mrs. Logg. "Kitty and I are going out for the moving-picture show right now. Aren't we, Kitty?" She pried Miss Kitty's head off her shoulder.

Miss Kitty looked up and her old eyes were cloudy a moment before clearing. "Yes," she said. "A moving picture. With . . . who, Alice?"

"Joseph Cotten," said Miss Tibbitt.

"He's my favorite," said Miss Kitty.

"Well, good-bye, girls," said Miss Tibbitt. She and Miss Kitty staggered out the front door.

There was a dull thud from the bushes.

"Why," exclaimed Miss Tibbitt, "that cat stole one of the grapes off my shoes!"

The sound of their footsteps was swallowed in the rush of wind that came off the emerging river.

Abruptly the sun was overcome by a cloud. The already twilight of the parlor sank into even darker shadow.

Mrs. Logg's knitting needles clicked furiously. In the dimness rare shafts of light caught on their copper color, fast-moving. They shone like thin blades of fire in her ancient hands.

I stood up from my stool and straightened my spine. I walked to the window.

Soon, I knew, in another month, the snow would be drawn once more into the soil, and spring would be upon Chaucy. I traced with my finger a wet line in the bare and thin coating of frost which clung to the window.

Spring. The low and wet green murmurings of it were on the wind of winter. They lingered beneath the unthawed soil. The branches of tall and slick trees hid buds within them, small, like tiny hands folded, buds rich with hidden layers and tender sweetnesses. Green spring when the hills lifted from their basins, and the shadows of birds moved among the leaves, their soft and shrill cries carried on the winsome air of the season. They flickered like ghost things. They glistened like sprays of light thrown out by a whimsical sun. In the night their forms, like phantoms, blew across the moon.

I pressed my nose flat against the chill, damp windowpane. The room was heavy with the smell of Mrs. Logg. I could hear the clatterings of pans, and the shutting of the door as Mrs. Turncew left our house. It was the smell of old medicine, kept locked away and behind bottles in the medicine cabinet, let loose on the world after a period of ten, perhaps fifteen years. It was the smell of fire, of wool slightly wet, of old lady's hair.

My hand lingered on the sill. Then I withdrew it.

With a great groan, Mrs. Logg stood and extended each extremity of her body, one at a time. She pulled her dress bosom down.

"Well," she said, rubbing her wet forehead, running her finger down its deep wrinkles. "I think I'll go up and catch me a nap."

She eyed the moose head disapprovingly. He leered back at her.

With a waddling motion, she headed grimly toward the stair.

I sat down in her chair. It was slightly damp with the sweat of her. It was too soft. I started to stand up. I heard a noise. I stood up and walked toward the window. I stopped in the center of the darkening room.

"Em." It was Uncle's voice, from very far away, in the bath-room.

"Yes," I said. I put my hands on the arm of the chair and stared at them. A very deep silence.

"Once," said my uncle, "when I was young, younger than you, and we had the farm outside Marion, I came to town to board a bus, travel here, see my father. I was in the bus station, me and my older cousin Bonney, and we had to go to the bathroom. Worse than anything . . . we had to. So Bonney and I, we decided to find the outhouse. Only we couldn't." He paused, and I could almost see him opening his hands out wide. I nodded. It was like he could see me nod. "There wasn't any, you see. Bonney and I had never seen a . . . toilet. Only outhouses, slop jars . . . We came to this room—it said 'Kings.' The other said 'Queens.' So we went in, and there was this toilet sitting there. It was the water-closet type, with this closet up tops, and you pull on the rope, and the water falls down. That's what flushes it."

I nodded again.

"Well." His voice drifted far away. "I said to Bonney, 'Bonney, is this one of these commode things?' And Bonney said, 'Reckon so.' So we tried it. . . . I tried it, and Bonney, he said, 'This rope thing, Carl, what's it for?' And he pulled it. All this water fell down; a little door opened in the bottom of the water closet, and the water fell right down in the toilet. Practically drowned me. Bonney and me run so fast you could scarcely see our dust, and hid behind the hardware building. We thought we'd broken the thing."

There was a long pause.

"My wife, Emmeline . . ." began Uncle Lamb. "Emmeline," he said, "Emmie. Emmie, I can't come out now. I don't know what to do. I can't come out. . . ."

Outside the twilight ripened into night, and the stars, like little buds, unfolded.

It seemed an eternity before I heard his voice breaking across my silence.

"Em," he said, "do you ever think sometimes that maybe

this world is just the inside of a big blue bowl, and the stars are only pinpricks in the bowl?"

I nodded, and put my hand out to pull the curtain.

"Em . . ." he began. He stopped.

CHAPTER *Seventeen*

Ancient trees gave birth to the voluptuous balloons of blossoms I remember cradling in my hand—the bulge of tulip-tree blooms which fell to melt into the earth, all thick with rot. Spring passed.

Southern Indiana is beautiful in spring. The season rolls down to become the bubble hills, round and emerald and fragile, like breath-blown balls. They are ripe with color, broken by the somehow velvet brownish-blue of the many small and winding streams that cut it with their flow, and give themselves, like ladies of easy virtue, to the greater, more worldly White River.

The land is enchanted. It seems as if one day, in the far-ago and unknown past—the day when land swam from the center to bubble and froth—God's hand passed, and the land froze in its contortions.

But this suspension of movement, like all things of God, was temporary. Standing on the dainty hills, I felt as if at any moment the thin swell of hill beneath me would thaw, and the hill slide back into itself, deflated, while the remainder of the land seethed and exploded.

In the clear-eyed iridescence of morning we brought the wicker chairs out onto the porch once more and sat, from morning until the night, when dark threw its first shadows across our summer faces.

Uncle, to avoid further skirmishes with the omnipresent Mrs. Turncew, stayed in the bathroom nearly all the time.

When Mrs. Turncew moved her heavy mahogany bedstead in—it resembled a Gothic cathedral, highlighted by gargoyles done after a likeless of Abraham Lincoln—Uncle moved Grandfather's West Point army cot into the bathroom. He moved it out for one day to be fumigated—it was upon this selfsame cot that my grandfather had entertained the numerous chickens of yesteryear.

On the few occasions that Uncle ventured forth, it was always with the assurance from me that Mrs. Turncew had departed for Orphro's Grocery, or to Amberson's to buy new eyes for the halibut in Miss Tibbitt's room. But now, with spring in its grave and summer upon the land, Uncle felt the great urge to be out and on the chicken coop.

Uncle had always loved summer—or rather Uncle had always enjoyed summer. He hated it actually. It killed his peonies.

Uncle had always kept peonies. He had twenty peonies scattered in a somewhat hysterical pattern in and amongst the various other flora that ran rabid in our front lawn. They began at the walk and continued in an orderly fashion for two, perhaps four, flowers. Then one delinquent broke ranks and scurried over to the opposite end of the yard next to the porch rail, where it glowered with blood hatred at its more respectable fellows. The rest of the peonies, being possessed of the sense of purpose of sheep, wove drunkenly between the two extremes. They adhered neither to the established trio that smugly lined the walk, nor to the single angry peony that hid in the shadows of the porch and hissed.

Summer in its early sweetness gave birth to the peonies. They swam from their stalks into the velvet air to blossom in slow and sensual luxury under a sun not yet brassy with its age. This sun smiled gentle on the peonies in this, their first hour. As time drew on, it gave rise to the ants.

They sprang, hundreds of them, from the soil, and squatted

upon the peonies, insolently chewing their feelers despite all my uncle's attempts to unseat them from their pink heaven.

The sun, growing in her fury, became obscure in the sky. It blended into a white ball of fuzz and sent out airy fingers, while my uncle sat asleep on the chicken coop, to strike each one dead as an undermilked cow. After this dastard act it drained them of any water they might possess.

Their petals grew paper-thin, waxy, and their extreme softness bore the traces of rot in the brown that circled and cut across them in jagged lines.

Eventually the peonies keeled over in protest, and Uncle Lamb was obliged to mow them up. Which he did. The year before, while he was stalking up and down the front lawn, the metal and rusted blades of the lawnmower seizing, then cutting, each bruised and near-white stem, Uncle had turned a corner to accommodate the route that the ambiguous peonies had taken, whereupon foot met metal and rusted blade—an act that the blades promptly obliged by chopping up Uncle's toes.

Uncle lost two toes, two halves of toes, one fourth of toe, and managed, by some saving grace, to retain the little one as a reminder of the fully appendaged glory that had once been his foot.

Feeling the burn of summer upon the land, the blood, and the toe that we had never recovered from the front lawn after the accident, called out to him: come, see. Summer is burning bald the trees, a new wealth of peonies, and summer is siphoning life from them. Summer is casting the town in yellow haze. Come sit atop the chicken coop!

He had, summer after dry, scorching summer. He had surveyed the weight of its hand upon Indiana. It was a season he could feel, a sensation he could hold and knead in his hand— this hatred, this fierce, contemptuous love for summer that he cherished.

Summer was Indiana more than any one other season, more

than winter with its amnesiac cold, or spring with its decep-
tive sweetness. It was only the monster that delicate spring
gave birth to that was real. Because he was of Indiana, Uncle
was of summer. His mother, his lover, his hate, his solace . . .
In this one moment, his life crystallized and he could hold it
—a tangible thing—in his hand. The draw of summer pulled
him out of the bathroom, sometimes even when Mrs. Turncew
stalked. I could see his shadow slipping along the dark corri-
dors of the house, through the narrow shafts of sunlight with
which summer pierced the atmosphere.

CHAPTER *Eighteen*

The weather galvanized Mrs. Logg into a fever pitch of good works. Counting her days as numbered, she made the resolution to do as much as was humanly possible to turn my child's mind onto the right track.

She had ceased the Bible readings the morning in late April when she had run into the Song of Songs—having perused it, she decided it improper for any lady to read. "It was only put in to sell the book," she said, and laid the Bible back on the sofa side table.

Casting about for something else, she chanced upon the window in the parlor one afternoon. What she saw through it was horrifying.

Mr. Rose was drinking spirits in his living room next door.

Mrs. Logg's first thought was for my welfare. The next hour found her atop a straight-back chair, nailing the curtains of the living room shut and to the wall.

Uncle poked his head out of the commode. "And what," he said, "do you think you are doing with my parlor curtains?"

Mrs. Logg turned around on the chair—an undertaking in itself. The chair sagged in the middle, and the cane bottom strained almost to breaking. Mrs. Logg pointed over to the Roses'. "Mr. Rosenblum is being disgusting in his parlor," said Mrs. Logg. She turned back around and with vigorous blows wedged the nails into the wall.

Her statement seemed to cover the subject. Uncle retreated back into the commode.

When the actual nailing had been accomplished, Mrs. Logg drew me aside and told me explicitly just what I was not being witness to through the window.

The practices of the Rose-nblum (Mrs. Logg declared that since only Jews drank spirits, therefore the Roses were Jews, therefore they had changed their name from Rosenblum, and shouldn't someone tell the Reverend Mr. Fitz-Simons over at the Congregational?) family were detrimental to my puerile psyche. The Rose-nblums held wild pagan rites in the various rooms and corners of their dark house. Mr. Rose-nblum—oh, he seemed to be a quiet, good man, but he was a seething pot of iniquity, a man diabolical. He was a man who would not hesitate to drink wine in full view of his parlor window, therefore in full view of our parlor window, therefore in full view of me standing at our parlor window—God forbid.

What effect upon me this spectacle of debauchery would have had I do not know. Mrs. Logg watched me with great apprehension, lest at any moment, if left to my own resorts, I should bound to the parlor window, plaster myself against its rippled frame, and hastily realize, in the form of the wicked Mr. Rose-nblum, the model for my future behavior.

The blockage of the parlor window was one safeguard. Others were forthcoming. Mrs. Logg was constantly on guard against losing one of God's creatures—which, being under age, I was.

Shortly after nailing the curtains to the wall, Mrs. Logg, ever the watchful guardian of my soul, woke up one morning to the disturbing realization that, while I couldn't see the house, the house was still there.

In regard to my future purity of heart, of mind, of body— already well insured, I thought, as Mrs. Logg had fitted me out that year with long black sateen bloomers, reaching nearly to the knee and sufficient to at least discourage, if not acutely terrify, any viewer of my nether limbs—Mrs. Logg was ever ready with initiative. She took some plumber's chalk and drew a wavy blue line on the crack in the sidewalk on the boundary line between our house and Mr. Rose-nblum's.

"Avoid this line, Mary," she admonished. She waved the piece of azure chalk at me. She added in an exceedingly grim tone, "Step on this crack, break your mother's back."

This did not particularly faze me.

My mother had been dead for lo these many years. Any breakage of her back would have but more speedily insured her return to dust—if indeed she had any backbone left.

This thought provided much ghoulish speculation for a number of days.

Content with the wall she had created between Mr. Rosenblum and me, Mrs. Logg put away the plumber's chalk and settled back on the chicken porch to watch the season as it uncurled and lazed in the streets. But Evil was not so easily conquered.

A week after Mrs. Logg had first drawn the line with the plumber's chalk, Mr. Rose-nblum came out of his house. He nagged the soil around his front step, kneeling to favor it with white fertilizer, wrenching from it the high-growing weeds. He paced out his lawn twice, steeped in criticism for its burnt and anemic appearance, and then he watered it. The lawn. It was an act which brought instant water death to Mrs. Logg's plumber's chalk line.

Mrs. Logg—inflamed with anger at this blatant attempt to lure me over to his, the dimmer, side of morality—defiantly seized the plumber's chalk and waddled out to kneel in the warm sun and re-create the bounds between me and sin.

CHAPTER Nineteen

It was just about that time that the Great Happening occurred.

The Great Happening happened at the place of the Second
Coming—a locale much exalted and publicized by its full-
color immortalization on the back of that year's stock of fans,
courtesy of Boxwright Brothers' Funeral Supply and Co-
operative.

Upon the back of this worthy fan were depicted, in Mrs. Ellender Lobbin's cabbage patch, Mrs. Ellender Lobbin and
Jesus Christ.

It had occurred one fine and sun-filled morning in early
May that Mrs. Ellender Lobbin was just puttering around in
her cabbage patch, tending things, weeding, pruning, patch-
ing, doing whatnot, and all of a sudden Jesus Christ appeared,
eating a Fig Newton, and said unto her, "Hello."

Mrs. Ellender Lobbin had five children. She had one two-
year-old sister. She had an aging maiden aunt. This is not to
mention a husband not well versed in the world of work. Mrs.
Lobbin seized her maiden aunt Junie's new Polaroid off her
neck and took one, two, three pictures of Jesus Christ at His
Fig Newton just like that.

In some five minutes the pictures were ready for Jesus to au-
tograph. Which He did very graciously. Whereupon Mrs. Lobbin, realizing the social prestige involved, invited Jesus in for
a taste of sugar tea and some almond macaroons.

Jesus, who had just had that Fig Newton, declined the invitation, saying, "Another time, maybe?" He wandered off in the direction from which He had come.

Before His head had been swallowed into the horizon, Mrs. Lobbin had called up the radio station in Mt. Vernon with an advertisement for genuine autographed photographs of Jesus Christ as He appeared in Mrs. Lobbin's cabbage garden. They sold like the proverbial hotcakes.

CHAPTER *Twenty*

And slowly and very sweetly the days passed, each disappearing before the other's approach. Each soft night was the blowing out of a tiny candle. The river swam in slow luxury toward its Mississippi end. The birds, shadows in the dark bowels of newly leaved trees, I heard but did not see—ghosts of substance.

There was a hitch to it all, a hollowness that marked the long days and the fiery nights. There lingered over the days a difference, a narrowness, an emptiness. They came, they died, days. And they melted, not as days lived melt, but as days filed away for some future end blend one by one into each other. The drone of the bees lay heavy on the air. Suddenly the river's flexible voice turned to nonsense and babbled like some idiot in my ear.

I could feel it. I felt it all round. Heat rained down on the town. Stumbling across my mind, I would find it blank—some skull-encircled vacuum, buzzing, always buzzing, taking on a cry of bees. My shoulders grew heavy with it—the hollow sleeping, the hollow waking, the hollowness of being awake.

I took to eating rummies. By the thousands.

The rummies man lived on the other side of the schoolhouse. His dim and narrow establishment was located in what might have been called Chaucy's shopping area—abloom as it was with a hardware store; an Eli Lilly pill warehouse, graced on top by the squatting and secret-holding apartment of Mrs. Bird; a barbershop; a Beautyrama; the diner; the House of Chaucy; the Steamboat Bill; a Kress's five-and-dime; Amberson's; Boxwright Brothers'; and a dank and evil-smelling drugstore, which he called a candy shop. I don't know whether it was or not. I never saw any of the merchandise closely enough to be capable of ascertaining whether or not this was true.

When you were uptown it sprang out at you like a finger of darkness in the block. It was a place where you ventured with pennies in your hand. It was a place where you stood and waited for that mysterious and wonderful shift of light to take place within your eyeball, so that you could dimly make out forms and objects.

The shop was about two children high, one fat child wide, and the windows that crowned it were thick with the dust of many years. The rummies man had a long hook with which he attacked the windows at infrequent intervals, tearing away from their sills the accumulated grease and dirt.

The rummies man himself was somewhat of a phenomenon. He was very tall, too tall for his child-size shop—a fact for which he compensated by stooping a full two or three feet. He was also thin—so loosely fitted together that his bones rattled in the overlarge sockets of his skeleton.

Whether he was dark in complexion or light I never could tell. I never saw him outside his shop. But his pupils were tiny and dark in his face, stamped on very large, ball-round eyeballs that were white as a field of snow before the rabbits had set their early-morning mark across it. Tiny and speedy, the pupils rolled and gyrated.

He never blinked. He could sit and let flies walk over his eyes. They were large, hairy, black flies—it looked as if his eye had monstrous, seething growths on it. He said it was aborigine blood flowing in him.

Other than the fantastic eyes, I remember the rummies man

hardly at all except that he had a narrow, pigmentless mouth —it seemed almost flat in his face—and a nose that snaked its pencil thinness in an irregular journey down to meet with his lips. These were only the high places to his face, those which captured the meager light of his shop and held it. Of the darker, more cadaverous pockets of his incredible visage, I know nothing. His face appeared out of the darkness only to ask for my money. It folded as quickly back into darkness.

You always had to have a reason for existence, Mrs. Logg taught me, some accomplishment that, when practiced, aided this world. There were two reasons that the rummies man was entitled to life.

The first was that he could, without so much as a single wince, draw a silk scarf in one ear and out the other.

The second was that he made rummies.

The rummies man sat in the back of his toothpick of a shop, and from the darkness that lay thick and unyielding in that portion of the candy store—even my adjusted eyes could not pierce it—brought forth rummies.

I could hear him as I stood waiting, later sitting on one of the numerous orange crates, my knees spread out wide, my palms moist.

There was a roll of wheel, it seemed to me. Above the brisk shushing of its sound, I could make out the snatches of the rummies man's song:

"Let the farmer praise his grounds,
 Let the huntsman praise his hounds,
 And the shepherd his sweetly scented lawn.
 But I, more blest than they, spend each night and happy day
 With my charming little cruiskeen lawn, lawn, lawn, lawn,
 O, my smiling little cruiskeen lawn.

 Immortal and divine, great Bacchus, god of wine,
 Create me by adoption your son
 In hopes that you'll comply

That my glass shall ne'er run dry,
Nor my smiling little cruiskeen lawn, lawn, lawn,
Nor my smiling little cruiskeen lawn."

In the dim shop his voice would swell. It was a light voice. Toward the end of the song he would accommodate for the high notes by switching into a shrill falsetto.

It seemed a wonderful song to me. I wondered, sitting there, the pennies hot and sticky in my hands—so sticky that I wondered in the back part of my mind sometimes, whether I would open my hand one day and find the coins gone gooey, like penny chocolates—what the fascinating little cruiskeen lawn was.

Because of the wheel sound, I always imagined the rummies man to be sitting, like the girl in Rumpelstiltskin, at a spinning wheel, spinning out rummies.

The rummies themselves were long, narrow, shiny, very sticky brown-colored tubes, composed of molasses and something else that gave them a special sort of rich flavor. You could buy eight pin-narrow ones for a penny. If you were especially careful and allowed your mouth to water only a little, holding the rest inside or swallowing often, you could suck on one for at least twenty minutes.

I sat in the rummies man's shop and waited for him. Outside stood the hills, which had billowed and frolicked in the sweet air of spring a month and a half before. The sun had turned harlot; the grass world was burning away.

CHAPTER *Twenty-One*

The days spent in the bathroom grew torturous to Uncle Lamb in this July. Outside summer swam, gray and slimed—silent, like a velvet-hided octopus. It had settled firm over Indiana, encasing the whole of the state in one wet and slippery shell.

Within the bathroom I could hear the slow, even, monotonous pacing of Uncle Lamb's captive feet. In the atmosphere of summer, the sound of Mrs. Turncew's shrill scraping on the window of the bathroom cut sharp into my brain. All around me it seemed as if there was sound—a full foot or more from my ears, but nonetheless there, almost following itself—an osmosis of sound, of bees, of old ladies, of footsteps, footsteps, scratching, footsteps. . . .

My breath came slowly. It was as if I had to reach open with my mouth and bite off the air as it lay about me, as if I had to digest it for the oxygen content. It was heavy, sodden with water. Time and sensation were thickened and weighted. All sound was so far away, so muffled. It was as if all movement of everything was up, up in the sky where God sat and hoarded all the wet behind a high and impossibly remote wall of clouds that rose pure, innocent of rain.

Flat-handed windmills stood turning, cutting the air, soaring—their spikes caught on the frayed ribbons of blue laced into the gray of burnt sky.

The ladies, Miss Rama, Mrs. Logg, Miss Tibbitt, and Miss Kitty, sat and, like lumps of fried dough that have begun slowly to sink into themselves with the oppressive elephant heat of summer, beat furiously at the air with their artillery of fans and pamphlets.

In slow, sugary rivers their moisture ran out from them and stayed in tiny, dark grease spots on the slightly damp floorboards of the porch.

I lay belly-flat on the porch swing with my nose wedged tight in one of the slats, watching with uninterested eyes the battle royal between the slow movement of the swing and the sunspots the lattice threw onto the wooden floor. Reaching up from under the swing, I wedged a rummie through the slat, catching it in the curl of my tongue.

The sound of the pacing stopped, then started again—back, a pause, forth, a pause, back and forth, a pause, and back.

I tried to concentrate on the sunspots.

"I see now," said Miss Rama. She assaulted the large and exceptionally hairy bee that hung drowsily on the air and that, fanned to life by the rapid flutterings of her church pamphlet, was making periodic passes at her ear. "I see now where they've got a standard coffin. Made out of top walnut. Burgundy lining. Velvet, of course. Quilted."

"Oh?" asked Miss Tibbitt, brightly lifting the cover off the birdcage and jamming between the wires a somewhat jaundiced piece of lettuce. Glorio jammed it right back out again. "I do think that idea of Nellcine Turncew's is so commendable. Sister writes me that they buried young Bowie in one of those model ones you're talking about, Rama. Young Bowie, you know, her son? Sister was not pleased at all. Not at all. The undertaker, Mr. Crabster from Wapingers, come up to her on the very night Bowie was dying, and he talks her right into buying that model coffin. Standard, you say? And Sister, well, she's hardly in any position to argue. It was her Hour of Grief."

A munching from the cage.

"But later, with the distraction wore off, and Bowie all laid out in that shoddy affair, Sister took herself off to the parlor and looked at it. Inferior quality?! Very inferior, and the finish was bad. Little linseed oil, and that was the better part of it." Miss Tibbitt shook her head disapprovingly.

"You don't say," said Mrs. Logg. "Well, there's no four ways to it. Nellcine's idea is the best of all. I've been thinking I'll get me a coffin as well. I just might do that."

Miss Rama swatted at the great hairy bee that hung suspended in the air. "Shoo, you buzzard!"

The bee elevated itself at Miss Rama's violent attack and slid insolently through the atmosphere to the porch post. There it settled and proceeded to give Miss Rama the eye.

The pacing stopped. It started. There came a shrill scraping on the windowpane. I could hear in the distance the dim bleatings of Mrs. Turncew as she called my uncle's name softly through the window. Then I heard the dim padding of her feet as she scurried back around to the kitchen.

We waited for summer's cool.

Summer's cool was an elusive season and known only to Indiana. It was born off the bright blue waters of Lake Michigan. It sprang like some green gauze Venus from the sea, and, born of water, it sped down the map of the state, like a vital grandmother trying, in the course of a single summer, to visit all her children. She stopped in Delphi, in Wabash, at Kokomo. She finally reached us in the crotch of the state in August, when she fell into a lavender faint on one of Uncle's plump peach coverlets.

We comforted her. We heralded her coming with pickled lemon slices, with Cat's Tongue Touch Macaroons. But, revitalized, she seized her satchets of sweetness about her and ran the train back to Gary.

Without her, scent stayed where it was born, deep within the blossom of the honeysuckle. To smell, you had to seek. To seek, you had to risk the familiarity of large, exceedingly hairy bumblebees. They hung, the children of summer, suspended in the butter thickness of sky. Their sound rolled out from them and flattened, spreading in an endless wave to meet with our ears.

I lay in the porch swing, with my nose in one of the slats, and the porch swing slid, cutting space. The light grew out from the electric bulb of sun.

Rather than seek, I waited for summer's cool to pull open the buds with efficient hands and throw the scent of summer all around me, and for her touch to give color to the dawn.

Out of the corner of my eye I watched Mrs. Logg's bosom as I lay. It swelled; it climbed. It blossomed out from her formidable frame, emerging like some night animal from too small a lair. It crouched on her, and sitting, it deposited the end of itself on her bulbous knees, and lay, a breathing and ominous thing.

I thought of Verbena's bony chest, where like twisted pieces of taffy the beginnings of breasts were stuck. I looked at my flat chest. I looked at Mrs. Logg. I pressed my body hard into the wood of the swing to discourage any action on my chest's part.

I settled my nose back into the deep and piney recesses of the wood once more. This in itself was a rather delicate art. One had to be equipped with a somewhat aquiline nose, for my grandfather had built the porch swing with the slats extremely close together, with the idea in mind that if he didn't, he might some day chance upon his chickens, driven by demon curiosity and that certain lack of brain power that so characterizes the chicken, all lined up, their heads thrust through the cracks of the porch swing, their pale bodies swinging heavily on the air, all quite hanged.

The bee shifted positions and gave me the eye.

From a bag sitting cooled in the shadow of the swing, I plucked another rummie and wedged it through the crack.

The pacing stopped, then was resumed.

"You eat any more of those candy sticks," observed Mrs.

Logg darkly, "and you're going to gain weight and be stuck in that swing forever. Your nose is going to swell up." She smacked her lips. "Until you die." She smiled.

Miss Tibbitt crammed the piece of lettuce in the cage once more.

Glorio crammed it out.

July's sun was raped clean of the protective, sweet mist of rose that surrounded spring's virgin light, and it burned, a brass and copper whore in an ancient sky.

The porch swing sliced slowly and painfully through the atmosphere; the sound of its movement was sodden with the weight of weather.

From the other side of the house, I heard the hesitant padding of feet as Mrs. Turncew made her way once more on this summer's day to the bathroom window to scratch at Uncle's solace.

"Lamb," she called softly. "Lamb?"

The street was like a mirror on which the shadows of leaves swam and glided heavily, their patterns like the shifting of a tired body. In the thick dark of its shade, the street seemed heavy-limbed, gray-voiced.

It was impossible not to think of Uncle as he had been before, in years before. I thrust my nose even further down into the scraping wood, but neither this, nor the voices of the ladies breaking off into silence, nor the bees, could drown out his pacing. It was as if his feet sank into my dulled brain with every step that he took, caught, imprisoned, back and forth . . . Uncle on top of the chicken coop; Uncle surveying the vengeance wreaked by earlier summer's wantonness, his beer can pressed into the folds of his stomach; Uncle smoking an occasional black and unctuous cigar, whose clouds of rich, ebony smoke swam out of him and solidified on other summer's air.

"Mary, will you get your nose out of that slat?" asked Mrs. Logg. "Do you want to ruin it?"

I reached with my long arm for another rummie and stuffed it through the tiny gap to my mouth. I put one hand on the lukewarm boards of the porch and gave it a half-hearted push that didn't seem to disturb its inertia at all.

"Get your messy hands off that board, Miss Mary," exclaimed Mrs. Logg. "Do you want to bring flies?"

The flies, at this suggestion, wove drunkenly in, and in solemn file lumped their great, hairy bodies down upon the small smudges of rummie I had left with my fingers on the floor. The sound of their buzzing was muted and sodden.

"Mrs. Logg," I said, struggling to get my nose out of the slat. I jerked it out. "My name isn't Mary. It's Emmeline."

"And look, girls," hissed Miss Rama. "Here comes Marble Freshower."

All the ladies stood up and waved gaily. "Hello!"

All the ladies sat down.

Miss Rama looked after her, cutting the air brutally with her church pamphlet. "Papist," she muttered.

Mrs. Logg rearmed herself with her fan, and methodically began rearranging the air with it. "I know," she said. "I know that your name is Emmeline. I'm aware of that fact. I have always known it."

I picked up my bag of rummies and put them on the swing. I began to pick the dirt out of my toenails.

Miss Rama gasped. "Emmeline Lamb! You've been out in the yard in your bares!" She was referring to my feet. "In your bares! How many times have I told you to never go out in your bares! You're going to catch your death in hookworms! Mind my saying now, hookworms surer than anything except God's wrath!" She blinked her eyes in disbelief. "And besides," she said, fanning herself violently. "It's immodest!"

"For a long time," said Mrs. Logg, rearing back and inspecting the line cut by her stocking into the flesh of her leg, "I have known that your name was not Mary. For a long time, but," she added sagely, "it should have been." She pulled at the bottom of her drawers. "I know your name," she continued, "as well as I know my own. It is for your own good that I call you Mary. It is," she scratched her mighty edifice of bosom, "for your own good. Now mind you, I'm not saying that being named Mary will get you into the Kingdom. No. Not the camel through the eye of the needle, nor the rich, no, nor you. Only you and your deeds on earth"—she looked significantly at Mr. Rose-nblum's house—"will get you in there. But it helps. It helps. My mother's name was Mary. My grandmother's name was Mary. My name is Mary. It was Mary Cline. That was until I married Mr. Logg. Then it was Mary Logg."

"What happened to Mr. Logg?" I put a rummie into my mouth.

"Oh, he died," said Mrs. Logg comfortably.

"Oh."

Mrs. Logg rocked back and forth, so vehemently that I thought the chair would soon just continue backing until it fell over. "And of course," she said, "my three daughters were named Mary."

"All of them?"

Mrs. Logg gave me a baleful look. I stuffed another rummie into my mouth and chewed vociferously.

"And my granddaughter was named Mary."

"How old is she?"

"She died."

"How?"

"Blood poisoning."

I swallowed my rummie. "How did she get the lead poisoning?" I asked. "Uncle sat down on a pencil once. He got lead poisoning."

Mrs. Logg looked at me scornfully. "*Blood* poisoning," and her tone indicated the worlds of respectability between lead poisoning and blood poisoning, "is hardly procured in such a fashion." With a wave of her fan she dismissed my family and our humble methods of obtaining disease.

Miss Tibbitt raised the cover on Glorio's cage and glared at him. "Stop that eating! Stop it immediately!" She lowered the cover. "I don't know why he does that. The chewing. I . . . I wonder," she added in a tone of melancholy rumination, "if I have failed him." She settled back into her chair.

Miss Kitty picked up her fan and swatted at the air with it. She put it down and fell asleep again.

It occurred to me that I had not heard the scratching of Mrs. Turncew's brittle fingernails on the glass panes of the bathroom window for a considerable length of time. Then, from inside the house, I heard Mrs. Turncew's insistent, nervous shuffling, the various loud clatterings of pans and utensils.

"Where is your uncle?" asked Miss Rama. She ran her bony finger up and down her side; it caught momentarily in each of the small hooks of her corset. Miss Rama asked this question some six or seven times a day. She knew where he was. She stared at my feet with absorption. By now they were surely hookworm heaven.

"In the bathroom," I said.

Shadows, slowly moving in, blocked out the spots of sun the lattice had cast on the wooden floor. A bee's drone rose and fell on the flat air. It seemed as if, in that one moment, the whole world had slid into a notch in time, had stopped in its revolution, had been caught against its impulse. The leaves hovered on the brink of movement. The sun froze in its travels. The silence sat down upon each lady on the porch.

"Mrs. Turncew's in there," I said. I had to say something.

"In the *bathroom?*" exclaimed Miss Rama. Her face lighted up.

"In the kitchen," I said.

"Oh."

"She's making meringues."

"Oh."

"I don't think," I continued, "that Uncle much likes Mrs. Turncew."

"Emmeline!" exlaimed Miss Rama.

"He goes into the bathroom every time she comes," I said. Miss Tibbitt blushed.

"Well, he does! And he flushes the john so she won't think he's drowned or nothing!"

"Anything."

"Emmeline!" cried Miss Rama. "Whatever! When did you hear such a thing? What else did they say?"

I crammed another rummie into my mouth. "Uncle Lamb."

"Mr. Lamb!!" cried all the ladies with one voice.

"He says . . ." I observed. I took the rummie out of my mouth and ran my finger around its sticky body. "He says he prefers the chicken coop." I put my finger in my mouth.

"Oooh," said the ladies.

"Mmmm," I said. I nodded my head.

A pan crashed onto the kitchen floor, and I heard Mrs. Turncew's light, almost musical voice sing out, "Oh Lam-ab!"

"I'm brushing my teeth!" shouted Uncle Lamb. He flushed the toilet.

"It's a pity," said Miss Rama. "Nellcine makes simply lovely meringues."

"Laah-mamaba!"

Three violent flushes of the john shook the porch floor. The ladies all looked up in unison. A clattering, and the crash of the commode seat returning to its customary place of reposal, and Uncle Lamb appeared at the porch door.

I sat up.

Uncle zipped up his pants.

Miss Rama seized up her church pamphlet and vigorously swatted at the air.

There came from the kitchen a tremendous crashing of

pans, a muted slapping of pan holders, and the hollow sound of numerous plastic vessels being shoved unceremoniously aside, and Mrs. Turncew appeared at the parlor window, which opened onto the porch. She peered out and saw Uncle.

"Lamb!" she cried.

Uncle stomped onto the front porch, and Mrs. Turncew galloped behind him. Her nylon dress was this morning a shower of green and golden specks, dark under the arms with her reaction to summer's heat. She was armed with a plate whereon resided a goodly supply of sugaring, pink confections.

Uncle looked at her.

He straightened up and, swinging his great belly in the direction of the porch swing, sat down next to me. Even in the half light of the porch, I could see that Uncle's already-immense bulk had increased in size. His belly far overreached the lenient confines of his belt, and rolled and rolled again until his navel was completely obscured, hidden deep within the bulk of him. Light caught and lingered on the strange golden hairs that snaked from his bald pate. Seen against this yellow atmosphere, he looked like a cherub caught in hell when he wasn't looking. The sparse and ethereal fuzz illuminated his fat, rubber-pink face like some obscene halo.

Mrs. Turncew looked at us.

We spread.

She looked at the swing, somewhat aghast: except for two inches on either side of us, the porch swing was covered completely.

"There's a seat," said Uncle. He smiled. "It's over there."

Mrs. Turncew's face sagged for a moment. Then it rose back and became once more the original bulbous features. She began to bustle about. "Oh yes, of course, and if there isn't, and sakes, it's over there by dear . . . and isn't there? Oh my, well, how are you, Rama? And *who* would like one of Nellcine's meringues? *Lamb?*" She breathed.

Uncle gave the pink meringues the eye. He gingerly picked up the tiniest one.

Mrs. Turncew batted her ancient and brittle eyelashes until I thought that they would break off. "Emmeline?"

I gingerly picked the next tiniest one.

Mrs. Logg looked at me sinisterly. "What do you say to Mrs. Turncew?" she demanded.

"Thank you, Mrs. Turncew," I said. I handed my meringue to Uncle Lamb, who promptly stuffed both his and mine down one of the many holes of his T-shirt.

"Mary? Alice?" Mrs. Turncew hotfooted it around the porch, showering each lady with what Uncle referred to, muttering, as "parrot eyes." With what might have been termed a flutter in a woman two decades her junior, Mrs. Turncew settled herself down in the chair beside Miss Rama. She eyed Uncle.

"Well now," she said. "How do you all like my pinkies?" Her eyes swam over the porch, blindly catching on each face, springing to sudden, alarming life when they came to roost on my uncle's sullen visage. "Lamb?" she pounced.

Uncle grinned broadly. "They are now in the proximity of my belly button," he said. It was true.

"Oh!" cried Miss Rama, leaping up and clapping both her hands over my ears—an act which brought out of my mouth the rummie I was hotly in the process of emulsifying.

"Mary!" exclaimed Mrs. Logg. "There is no need to spit!"

"Emmeline?"

"Ma'am?" I pulled my ear back into shape.

"The idea of saying such a thing in front of a little child!" hissed Miss Rama at Uncle Lamb.

"How did you like your pinkie, dear?"

"Oh," I said. "It was really delicious. Thank you. Thank you." I stuck my finger in my ear.

"I'm so glad, sweetheart," said Mrs. Turncew. She reached

over and squeezed my knee so hard that all the blood ran out of it. "You like another one?"

"Oh, no thank you, ma'am," I said. The ladies glared at me. "I'd better not." I opened my mouth wide. "My teeth." I put another rummie in my mouth.

Mrs. Turncew looked at me. "Well," she said, addressing herself to the group at large. She looked at me again, and this time I detected a sort of concern playing in it. I massaged my knee to get the blood back into circulation. "Well, you simply wouldn't believe it! I was rummaging around in the pantry, looking for a cake plate, you understand—Lamb has been such an old *precious* . . ." Bat of old gray eyelashes. ". . . he's just letting me use his kitchen just any time I want to? Well, the *stove* is so much bigger. When we got our stove, my former husband and I? We were just two young things, come up from Louisville—Mary Logg, you know how poor the country is down around Lexington? A crow flying over'd have to carry a lunch. We bought us that small, itty bitsie stove and just never did get another one. While Lamb is sitting out on the chicken coop, I use it—really Lamb, I wish you wouldn't sneak up onto the chicken coop—the air just can't be healthy, and anyway I was in the pantry, and you'll never, you'll just never, never in a million years guess what I . . . oh, come on, Alice. No. Don't be a silly. You aren't *fat!*"

Uncle deftly reached inside his T-shirt and threw the two pink meringues over his shoulder into the honeysuckle bush.

"What was that?" asked Mrs. Logg suspiciously.

Uncle looked over his shoulder. He shrugged.

"Under the wringer washer," Mrs. Turncew continued. "Lamb, I do wish that you would throw out that wringer washer and get one of those Maytags. I just can't sleep at night!"

Uncle chuckled softly.

"I mean, *knowing* that you have that old wringer washer in

that pantry, and that—who knows? Emmeline might just one day run her arm through it!"

I looked at my arm.

"You laugh! You laugh! It's happened! It's happened, and it's ruined many a young girl's looks completely, too. And under that wringer washer was this picture."

Uncle blanched.

"Of a young girl. Who is that lovely young girl under the wringer washer, Lamb?"

Uncle looked startled. His face drew up into itself, and his hands remained where they had rested, on his knees. Then quickly he flexed them. "That young lady," he said after a moment's pause—his voice was odd, but coated in the former veneer of calculated dryness that it had always assumed—"is my sister, Emmeline's mother. Dead."

"Oh!" gasped Mrs. Turncew. The mass of small folds that constituted her aged skin slowly purpled. She batted one set of eyelashes furiously, a feat I had hitherto thought impossible. I handed Uncle a rummie and looked at him. I felt oddly strange, as if some growing plant of strangeness had suddenly taken root in me. Uncle shook his head without looking at me. Automatically I put the rummie carefully back in its grimy bag and stared down at it.

Mrs. Turncew looked from me to Uncle Lamb. She thumped herself on the chest. Squelching the strangeness which had welled up in me, I made an effort to look at Mrs. Turncew dryly. I didn't know what she was getting so upset for, I told myself. I knew my mother was dead. And yet the amazement of there being anything left of this woman whom I had never seen, whom I didn't remember, whom I had never really believed in . . . Uncle had destroyed all her pictures, Miss Kitty had once told me before Uncle could shut her up; it was as if his sister did not exist. Slowly, testily, I put the rummie in my mouth.

And I forced the feeling out of me, pushing it out my

mouth, and my eyes, and my ears, and the tips of my straining fingers. I felt the immense vacuum of normality seize the inside of me once more, the sun once more warm on my face, the hot, biscuit odor of Uncle Lamb beside me. A slight breeze cupped the spindle-thin honeysuckle vines in its pale hands and, lifting them, breathed their hidden fragrance.

"Oh, dear!" said Mrs. Turncew at length, looking at me out of the corner of her eye. She whispered, "How dreadful for the poor baby!"

I smiled at her and chewed voraciously.

"Has she ever seen the picture?" she whispered to Uncle Lamb.

"She's not going to see . . ." Uncle began.

"No!" I said.

Mrs. Turncew turned to me.

"No, I haven't!" I said.

"Emmeline!" said Uncle Lamb.

Mrs. Turncew sat back and looked at both of us. "Lamb," she said. "It's her mother's picture. She ought to . . ."

"She ought not to!" said Uncle Lamb. He stood up. Then he sat down again. "Mrs. Turncew," he said slowly. "Consider the child's feeling. We are content to have my . . . sister's portrait in effigy, as it were, in reposition under the wringer washer. It's a fit reminder of her days upon this earth. . . ."

"Now, now, now," ruminated Mrs. Logg, rocking grimly back and forth. "Now I agree with Nellcine, Mr. Lamb. The child should definitely see her mother's picture. In fact . . . in point of fact . . ." She belched softly. "I think it would be a commendable idea if Mary's mother's picture were hanging over Mary's little bed. She could be a guardian angel. When my mother was alive, her picture hung over my bed. It still does."

"Mrs. Logg!" said Uncle.

"I agree, too," said Miss Rama. "It shocks me, it truly does, Lamb, that you could have kept that picture from this child as long as you have. I think it should be brought right out from . . ."

"I didn't hide it!" protested Uncle Lamb. "Didn't you hear Mrs. Turncew? It was right under the . . ."

"Now that's a fibber," said Mrs. Turncew, wagging her finger at Uncle Lamb. "It was in a trunk behind the wringer washer with ER stamped on it."

"What were you doing in the trunk?"

Mrs. Turncew clapped her hand over her mouth.

Miss Kitty's heavy buffalo head rolled over onto her shoulder. She snored.

"Glorio, stop that chewing!" exclaimed Miss Tibbitt.

Uncle looked at me, and in the nervous twitching of his eye I could feel a strain. I looked at him, questioning.

"Why don't you go and get that picture right now, Nellcine?" asked Miss Rama, puffing and snorting. "I will not sit here another instant with that child not knowing!" She panted.

"I was looking for the cake pan!" said Mrs. Turncew.

Mrs. Logg glared at Uncle.

"Mrs. Logg," begged Uncle, "please, please think. Can you imagine the . . . the effect seeing this picture could have on the child?" He turned to Miss Rama. "Do you think that I, as her uncle, would deny her anything which would help and illuminate her way through life?"

"The eight-inch pans were already in the oven!"

"But this picture . . . Believe me, it would not do that. It wouldn't. This child," indicating me, "this child, this flesh of my sister . . ."

Miss Rama gasped.

". . . mother or no mother. I will not have this little face traced in lines of misery." He looked around. He finished grandly. "This child is one of the earth's flowers!"

I bit my toenail.

"One of God's lambs!"

Mrs. Logg looked at me skeptically.

"In all cases, the answer is no." Uncle looked briefly from lady to lady, his plump fingers beating a nervous tatoo on his stomach.

Mrs. Logg looked at him. "In all cases, the answer is yes," said Mrs. Logg calmly. "Go and get the portrait, Nellcine."

Treachery swelled in me. Go and get the portrait, my heart whispered. I bit off the end of the rummie and crushed it between my back teeth.

"No!" said Uncle.

"Lamb," began Mrs. Turncew hesitantly. "Don't you really think that it's a good idea?"

"No, I don't think so. Not at all!" He stood up.

"Yes," said Mrs. Logg doggedly. She rocked her chair determinedly.

Please, I thought.

Mrs. Turncew looked at Uncle and then at Mrs. Logg. She sat down. She stood up.

Mrs. Logg glared at her. "Very well," she said, "I'll do it myself!"

She hoisted her huge body out of the rocking chair; with a hand working through the thin and water-spotted fabric of her dress, she pulled up her drawers. She swung her mighty bosom toward the door and stalked into the house.

Uncle leaped up and followed her to the door, into the hall. Then he stopped. He stopped. He pulled the flesh of his stomach and kneaded it with his crusty hands. He didn't look at me.

From the sound of pots and canisters yielding to Mrs. Logg, we knew she had hit the kitchen. There was a clatter as she rammed into the wringer washer.

Uncle's shoulders tensed, and then, breaking a rummie in two, he slammed down the hall.

"Lamb! Lamb! Where are you going?"

"To the bathroom!"

CHAPTER *Twenty-Two*

Mrs. Turncew stood there for a minute, pondering on the thing she had done. Then, just as quickly, she leapt up and ran down the porch steps and began to scratch vigorously on the bathroom window. "Lamb! . . . LAMB! Do you hear me? Lamb, do you hear?" She beat against the windowpane.

Three loud flushes roared up from the commode.

Uncle appeared once more on the porch. His face was almost purple with anger. He stomped across the floor and down the steps. For an instant I thought that he was going after Mrs. Turncew. I sprang up. But he continued walking straight, out into the street.

Mrs. Turncew peered out from around the corner of the house, wringing her hands within her apron pockets. "Lamb! Lamb!" she called. She stared after his disappearing figure.

Mrs. Logg waddled out the front door, and with a great crashing and creaking of brittle paper thrust a roll of white portrait out before her. She caught me by the ear and sat me down on the porch swing. She took the roll and pressed it out with her two hands. She sat on it. Then, holding it down by its impudent edges, she called my attention to it.

Not that my attention had not been on it before.

My mother's portrait could have been called unique.

It could have been called any number of things.

It portrayed a youngish woman, poker-faced, attired in a low-cut, apple-green evening gown holding violent disagreements with the tone of her complexion—and winning. She was pinned like some jaundiced bug to what I recognized as the parlor curtains.

The cut of the bodice displayed to the world a fine array of bones which Nature had substituted for what, on another woman, in the same place, would have been a cleavage.

Her singularly narrow shoulders were at full mast—their height threatened her low-hanging ears with contact. But the most fascinating of my mother's features was the amazing eyebrow which crossed over her two eyes, extending the width of her face with no attempt at interruption above the nose. In a burst of wiry, curling hair it swept and curled and leaped and coyly broke ranks to slither down her face in a brittle, black corkscrew, some hairs of it meeting in places with the base of her nose.

I stared at it. I felt oddly disturbed; something unknown to me swelled up in me. It fell hard and silent, like the breaking of some mountain in a silent world. It wasn't love. It wasn't hate. It was just—breaking. I stared at the portrait with fascination. In spite of the scrambled, boned visage and the dark features, there was a certain delicacy to my mother, and even beauty in the long, burnished hair. The face and the body seemed to swell and become momentarily real. Then I shut it out.

"See now," leered Miss Rama. "This is a really fine portrait. See, the eyes follow you!"

I nodded and tried to shut it out.

Mrs. Logg, who had become, in this hour, a veritable crusader, seized me once more by my arm and dragged me after her, across the porch, into the cool, green-shadowed house. She took my mother with her.

There could be no denying that the eyes did follow you. They did. They followed me up the stairs and down the corridor and into my room.

Wielding a hammer and nail hitherto concealed in the vast

pockets of her dress, she hung the picture in the same frame that had previously held pictures of Jesus Christ, and a copious number of dead fish.

Even then the eyes followed you.

To the left of the bed.

To the right of the bed.

Under the bed.

Into the bed.

Under the blankets, under the sheets, under the pillows and the hot-water bottle.

They followed you.

I was sitting under the bed, breathing deeply of the darkness and dust-smelling air that abounded in those nether regions when Mrs. Logg, her Christian spirit diminished, left me alone in my mother's company. With such quietude as her aged and bloated body could manage, she crept out of my room, pulling the door softly shut behind her. Her ankles creaked all the way down the stairs.

I peered out from under the bed.

Mrs. Logg had gone.

I stood up and walked over to the window. I sat.

My room was old, and the paper on the wall was old, too—green with the buds of painted plants not yet opened. It was very small and narrow, reminiscent of a back hallway. The floor was rough and filled with splinters.

There were pieces of things missing off the furniture—the handles off drawers, the knobs off beds. The mirror was silver and scarred, and the sun threw ever-widening panels of sunlight across the floor. It was a warm room. You could smell the warmth.

Pulling the yellowed shades down halfway, I scraped away with my hand the bodies of last night's crop of dead bugs, victims to my light. They lay black, or so tiny as to have no color, on the window sill.

I looked at my mother. My mother looked at me.

And then in the corner, beneath the gleam of a diamond ring on her hand, I noticed for the first time the initials which Mrs. Turncew had said were on the trunk—ER.

CHAPTER *Twenty-Three*

Uncle bought the bush at the Evergreen and Tulip Tree Nursery.

It wasn't an evergreen. It certainly wasn't a tulip tree. In fact we didn't know what it was. Neither did it—it did things, like bloom and grow, strictly on impulse.

Like Verbena it was albino, and very large. Its bare and twisted skeleton was just barely sheathed in tiny, ragged blooms the color of white gone yellow with age—albino, perhaps from its early heartbreak.

When Uncle returned home after he had stalked off our front porch, the bush was staggering about the back of the Evergreen and Tulip Tree Nursery truck—they had not tied it down. It had been a scant two hours since the bush's tragic first love: one tendril of its wandering branches had taken up with the pant's fly of the second salesman in such an affectionate manner that, despite frantic efforts on the part of the fly's owner, they could not be torn asunder.

Uncle appeared on the scene just when this heaven-made union of bush and fly had endured sufficiently for the salesman to entertain wistful thoughts of, at some time, seeking solace in the commode.

Uncle acted with a resolution born of inspiration. Unflinching, he ripped the fly from the ill-starred salesman's trousers—an action that sent the salesman winging it for the outhouse.

When he returned to Uncle and the scene of his recent torture, he sold the large shrub to Uncle at discount, Uncle having, in his absence, grown passing fond of the anemic shrub, and more than fond of the possibilities it afforded him. Once planted in the one-time flower bed beneath his bathroom window, he reasoned, it would keep out the prying eyes of the world in general, and the prying eyes of Mrs. Turncew in particular.

The bush responded with an enthusiasm that was touching. Once imbedded in soil, its already-mighty frame erupted in branch. It sent out tiny, jointed fingers, and from these fingers other branches sprung. It reached out and described its boundaries, and grew to describe new ones. It swam out of its central trunk, spanning the window in a maze of twisted wood, covering it with branches, and, not infrequently, blossoming. Being albino, it was high-strung, and wont to burst into hysterical bloom at almost any moment.

Uncle loved the bush. Through the bathroom window he watched it, even slid open the lowest section and touched it. It was so large, so dense and wide that Mrs. Turncew could not creep through it to scratch on the window. It was a shield.

CHAPTER Twenty-Four

It was not until night, and Mrs. Logg's coming to grimly switch off my lights, that I realized the true artistry with which my mother's portrait had been executed. For it was then that the eyes came for me—two white orbs in the darkness, staring. Under the covers. Under the pillows and the covers. I could feel them, alive as me, and rolling around inside the bed with me, looking, following, warm, slick, wet, round.

I couldn't sleep.

I would lie there in the silent, water-like stillness of the darkened room and watch her watch me.

She had the advantage.

She was larger. She was longer. She was greener. Her eyes joined to mine in one long, invisible thread, unbreakable, which only allowed me perfunctory looks at my windows to determine whether or not Wolfman was coming in to get me.

It continued for several weeks.

Then slowly it dawned on me that Wolfman might in truth be Glorio in a poor rabbit disguise.

This realization made it necessary to look in the right as well as the left direction, out the window, and at the door which separated my room from Miss Tibbitt's via the bathroom.

Even this was bearable. I could sleep on my back with both my arms spread out to protect myself, provided the mattress was still allied territory.

Mrs. Bird had read us a story out of the Third-Grade Supplement. It was about giant red ants.

There were red ants, big and fierce, that would eat anything that they ran into—be it bush, be it bird, be it human. The latter case particularly worried me.

With a little application of logic it came to me that if these hideous creatures dwelt in Africa, where Mrs. Logg said no self-respecting soul would go, what was to prevent them from living in my mattress?

They were living in my mattress.

Night became hell.

My eyes, open as they were all night to all possible dangers, grew great and gray and rimmed with red. After a week and a half of fending off danger, the combined forces of the Wolfman on the right and the left, blind ants maybe, and my mother indubitably, I stumbled one day past the bathroom just about the time the door was opening to permit Uncle a peek at the world of the foyer.

"Emmeline," he said sharply, peering at me. "Have you been into Miss Tibbitt's vapor medicine again?"

"No, sir," I assured him. I would not have gone near Miss Tibbitt's vapor medicine for the world. I had no doubt in my mind but that it was blood.

"Well," he said, suddenly uncomfortable. "What's the trouble? You look right peaked."

I couldn't take it any more. I broke down and told him.

Uncle stood in the half light of the door, and the color from the bathroom fell green around him. Then awkwardly he reached out and took me in his arms, lifted me up, and carried me upstairs to my room.

He looked at my mattress, then at me, scooped it up in his arms, and dumped it on the floor. He took a large red crayon and marked on the springs in a large and sprawling hand, "Bengali."

I wiped my eyes.

"See this," he said. "It's . . . uh, Bengali."

I hiccuped from my sobbing, and nodded.

"BENGALI!" Uncle thundered. "It means . . . 'The plague upon you!' in . . . Swahili! In Swahili. That's a language. All African ants understand Swahili. They speak it, you know." He scratched under his arm. "It's a matter of pride. Now, when any ant smells such a concentration of crayon, ink, or the like, he will be able to tell this means 'The plague upon you' in Swahili. He'll beat it for the anthills. It's tribal rule. No ant will stay where the word Bengali is written. Not," added Uncle sinisterly, "if he cares for his life.

"Now," he said, "about Wolfman . . . where are those comic books! I'm going to burn them."

My comic books: dog-eared, syrup-stained, and stuck together—holy documents of daemon gods . . . "Burn Glorio," I suggested, seeking to eliminate one possibility without angering the werewolf nation.

Uncle clawed under his arm. He scratched his sweat-streaked forehead. Then he went downstairs and packed some grainy garlic in a damp, mossy-looking linen bag. He got two peanut-butter jars, shiny, freshly cleansed of their original entrails by the energetic Mrs. Turncew, whose sacred duty it was to save every jar coming under her jurisdiction—a duty that had rendered the pantry a sea of blank and glassy faces.

"Now," he said.

I nodded.

He opened the bag, and instantly the scent of garlic slithered from the gaping hole of it and ran for the corners like night animals shot with shafts of light. It hid in cracks of the room. I sneezed.

Deftly, Uncle stuffed the wad of garlic into the peanut-butter jars. He clamped the lids on, and with his powerful, thick-muscled arms and wrists, screwed them tightly. "There," he

[*139*

said. He breathed. He coughed. "These will fend off any were-wolf. Or wolfman." He hung one on the door pulley of the transom, and one on a nail in the window.

As an extra added precaution, he walked downstairs and got the largest of the numerous crucifixes that we had in stock.

It was nearly a foot and a half tall, foldable at the feet and the neck. For this reason I had never seen it for very long in a state that wasn't toes-meet-knees and head-meet-belly-button.

On that morning, when Uncle Lamb brought the crucifix up and spread it out before me in its full splendor, I realized once and for all that these things my uncle was doing for me would cleanse me from all danger. The crucifix was magnificent.

It was painted in a simulation of ivory and gold. The gold having worn off in spots, the crucifix, in the fourteenth year of its existence, resembled nothing so much as a pillar of white, alabaster-pure, which had received from some blasphemous hand a blow of aging ochre.

Jesus was smiling. In miniature, in exquisite miniature, you could discern each one of His teeth—a surprisingly cheery leer, considering the state of His body.

From His hands ran great lumps of gold. The nails that pierced His hands were gold. His head was wreathed in thorns of gold. From His crossed, pointed feet ran a large lump of what had once been gold, before it had chipped off and been swept away by the sporadic brooming of Lucinda.

The only other time I had seen it unfurled was once, four years before, when Mrs. Winslow had taken to mind to hang it on the dining-room wall. It had not stayed there long. Uncle declared that he couldn't eat with it up there bleeding, so he took it down, refolded it, and hung it once more in the hall closet.

"Now *that's* enough to scare anybody," said Uncle.

I nodded reverently.

"Even," said Uncle, ruminating, "even . . ." He looked at

the picture. "Even Arthur Murray." He paused. "A train con-
ductor!" he muttered. Then he picked up the garden shears
sitting on my floor, and pruned the wall forever of my mother.
With a hesitation he ran his hands over the initials at the bottom and then quickly rolled it up. He stuck it under his arm
and went downstairs. I never saw the picture again.

CHAPTER *Twenty-Five*

With the slow and sultry passage of July, I found myself seeing less and less of Uncle. I would pass the bathroom door each morning, several times during the day, once more at night. Sometimes he would call out—my step was lighter than that of the ladies, softer than the shuffling half-whisper of Lucinda's splayed feet. At those times his voice was faraway, removed, bottled; it was as if it was slowly draining somehow of the rich liquid that had once distinguished it. It seemed dryer now, thinner. The hard blows of midsummer sun flowed fast and brutal about me, and it sounded almost brittle. The sun silently battled.

Thwarted by the largesse of the bush, which set the bounds between her scraping fingers and the window that, with its glass panes and its hysterical front of erratic daisy flowers, shielded my uncle from her possessive eyes, Mrs. Turncew abandoned her impersonation of the Good Cook and took on all aspects of a watchdog.

She haunted the bathroom door.

She became a fixture in the hall just as she had become a fixture in the kitchen.

She sat with her eager eyes in the half light, and slowly, convulsively, clasped and unclasped her thick-veined hands.

The kitchen stood suddenly quiet, a memorial to the change of times. Pervading all the front area of the house was a tension, a sense of waiting.

My uncle would turn the water on.

Mrs. Turncew would start.

My uncle, with great creakings in his joints, would bend to pick a book from off the floor.

Mrs. Turncew would beg, "Lamb, are you all right?"

Uncle would blaspheme.

Mrs. Turncew would squeal.

It went on and on.

The slight, caved-in figure in the front hall.

The nervous, increasingly furtive starts and audible movements of my uncle in his lair. The quick night-animal sounds of hurry.

Then suddenly, the appearance of the large Victorian straight-back chair, placed just opposite the door. Dark, almost maroon-colored velvet, it had spots of an ancient stain strewed about its threadbare once-majesty. Cherubim locked in a togetherness born of wooden vines and carved, sophisticated edelweiss squirmed all over it.

In this apparition the dim and shadow-deepened Mrs. Turncew deposited herself and, by dint of many strands of pastel embroidery floss and a shiny five-penny needle, brought forth by painful cross-stitch some six panels of operatic sparrows; flimsy, fragile flowers; acorns only partially filled in to suggest shadows; and free forest creatures.

Ewe lamb, I thought on the swing. He chose David also his servant . . .

> He chose David also his servant, and took him from the sheepfolds:
> From following the ewes great with young he brought him to feed Jacob his people, and Israel, his inheritance . . .

Ewe lamb, I thought. *You,* Lamb.

We sat, waiting.

CHAPTER *Twenty-Six*

One day, while passing the bathroom door on one of my journeys to the porch, I chanced upon a time when the embroidering Mrs. Turncew had repaired to her own small and sadly neglected home to haggle with the Posey County Electric Power Company.

I had, in my pocket, some money I had gleaned from the egg-lady jar, dedicated, now that it had attained the sanctity of my rear pocket, to the purchase of a day's supply of rummies.

As I snuck by on somewhat tender feet—lest any lady suspicious of my motive in visiting the kitchen daily, at this appointed hour, should chance upon me in the throes of my criminal activity—I heard Uncle call out.

"Em?"

I stopped and with a fast hand I stuffed the money more firmly down into my pocket.

"Yes," I called back.

There was a pause.

"Why don't you . . . come in," he said. "Spare the time?"

I looked around for Mrs. Turncew. Then I quickly slipped into the room, shutting the door firmly behind me. I was somewhat surprised to find it not locked. It was as if he had been expecting me.

The bush reached halfway up the window, bathing the room in a curious dimness.

The bathroom consisted of a lavatory, a linen closet filled

with my uncle's old diapers and my own, and a stuffed fox terrier which fell out every time you reached for an old diaper.
It also had a small john that had long since lost its claim to
newness, and now, with the loss of its paint and its gain of
mold, was beginning to assume something of a jaundiced air.

"You going up to town?" he asked. He pointed awkwardly
at my hand, which still lingered on my pocket.

I snatched it away. "Oh, I thought maybe about going," I
said.

The window, built into the wall by my grandfather,
stretched from floor to ceiling. Before the advent of toilets in
the house, the bathroom had served as the taxidermic center.
(This is not to say that toilets did not exist. They did. But
Grandfather had no doubt that his irrational chickens would
someday breach the distance between their porch and the
more removed chambers of his castle, and, with all due
aplomb, drown themselves. Uncle, however, had no chickens,
and he was not attuned to the charms of the chamber pot. In
1949 the stuffing room witnessed the sovereignty of the
commode—an innocuous event which entailed a small, humble bit of white porcelain sneaking in on two feet and hastening to squat in the darkest and most extreme corner of the
room) The shadows it threw across the room were green and
long.

"I was wondering if you could do something for me," he
said. He was sitting on the commode, fully clothed. He looked
up at me, squinting in the half light, and then, with a gesture
of his hand, he beckoned me over.

I stood beside him. In the light his face was half green, like
dulled copper, wavy with the reflection of leaves on its large,
smooth surface.

"Some beer," he whispered. He looked around. "It's been a
long time. Between . . . beers. You understand?"

"Yes," I whispered.

"Now, I'll have to write you a note," he whispered. "You

give it to Mr. Parrott Mewborn down at Steamboat Bill's." He produced a piece of dirty, creased paper from his pocket. "Dear Parrott," he wrote, speaking the words and looking up at me with a nervous, uneasy smile. "Please give my niece Emmeline two six packs of Falstaff beer. It's all right. Lamb." He put his pencil back in his pocket. He handed me the note. "The egg-lady jar," he said. "There's money in the egg-lady jar."

The sun had sunk a little, and outside, with sudden fright, a bird took up her wild cry. Silence fell on the room. Bottle-green in this diminishing light, Uncle seemed no longer human, but dead. His head hung sideways toward me in the green world, and with a growing root of fear I stepped closer to the door.

His head dropped and swung against the plush flesh of his chest.

I opened the door quickly and stepped out of the room.

Mrs. Turncew sat there in her high-backed baroque chair. When I stepped out, the whites darted up from her darkened eyes and met with mine in anger.

CHAPTER *Twenty-Seven*

One day in late July Miss Kitty woke me up. Her wizened face appeared next to mine on the pillow.

Outside, the sun had not yet hardened, and the sky swam sweet with clear-eyed morning. From somewhere a bird called. It was very early.

"Morning, Miss Kitty," I said. "What do you want?"

"I think it's here, Emmie," she said. "She sent it to me, Runa did, oh, I don't know how many years ago. It was a long time."

She smiled at me. It was a small, sort of animal, smile, and with her thin and incredibly twisted fingers she picked at the corners of my bed.

"What did she send you?" I asked.

Runa was Miss Kitty's oldest, only-living daughter.

"In your papa's attic," said Miss Kitty.

"In Uncle's attic?" I asked.

"Your daddy's, child," said Miss Kitty. I had always found it odd that Miss Kitty, who was the oldest boarder we had, who had been with my uncle in the time of my mother, could not understand that Uncle was not my unknown father. "It's very pretty, Emmie, pink, what you would call—purple?"

"Yes, ma'am," I said. I was confused.

"You and me together. We two will go up to the attic. We'll find it now. You see?" She smiled again. Her shy smile.

An even, dry heat was beginning to spread over the floors of my room. Narrow fingers of lighter white crawled up my walls. I guessed it to be nearing six.

I dropped to the floor. My warm feet, on contact, made a small, wet sound on the boards. Miss Kitty took my hand in her cold, white one, and we left my room.

Miss Kitty was not dressed yet. She had a sort of nightshirt on, gleaned from her recent journey to the Alice Babcock Chaucy Hospital, which had replaced the Sisters of St. Stephen, due to the unquestionable fact of its Catholicism, and the general ineffectuality of its cures. It hit her half-way down her bony shank. It was once white, perfectly plain, and because of its unwillingness to cover her back regions, was covered by a poison-green terry-cloth bathrobe that raveled its way down to her ankles.

Her feet were sheathed in old—hairless in this, the twelfth year of their existence—slippers, the heels of which were nowhere to be seen.

Her hair, what there remained of it, she had tied back into a little wad at the back of her neck.

We walked quietly down the hall so as not to disturb anyone. From her room I could hear the intimidated, breathy snores of Miss Tibbitt, the sinister roamings of Glorio's *promenade de matin,* the click of his cloven hoofs against the hollow of pine floorboards.

When we reached the end of the corridor, melancholy and faintly musty in this hour new with dawn, we opened the slender attic door and mounted the stairs.

The attic smelled of yesterday's heat and a thousand paperback books. Toward the farther end of it, I could make out the small, square, open window that allowed into our attic a million tiny birds. The tree leaves brushed it now, and the scent was fragrant, teeming with the promise of later heat.

Miss Kitty went immediately to a trunk by the window. With her hands raised white and separate-fingered, she set the roosting birds onto wing. "I think it's here," she said. "Runa sent it to me a long time ago. I don't know how long ago now." She smiled and with her hands worked slowly through the piles of fabrics that lay in the trunk.

Chiffons (bare in places), greens, and light purples, and calicoes, and finally she found it.

I sat down on a stuffed elephant's foot.

She held it up to catch the sun. Instead it blocked it, and I could not tell, in the darkness, how it looked. She closed the trunk and laid the material down on top of it. With her hands she smoothed it out.

I leaned over to see it; catching the first hesitant fingers of sunlight that shyly swam across the floor, it pulled them to it.

It was pink—a pale, baby's pink—crepe, soft and slightly granular to the touch. It was like a whole beach of tiny, identical stones. Over its surface cavorted innumerable and savage butterflies, pink, deeper pink, deepening to almost a rose, the violent shades of purple.

"Ah!" she exclaimed softly.

The small fingers of fresh light shifted with the show of shifting leaves, lighting the taller planes of her face and casting the lesser ones in darkness.

"It's just as I remembered it, Emmie," she murmured. Her voice was rarely clear, muffled by old age. But now, soft as it was, it came almost birdlike from her pole of throat.

I looked at the butterflies with horror. They were large, too large for the delicate fabric. Their wings leered. They seemed almost monstrous in aspect. With a great swelling, they reared their ugly heads.

"Just perfect," said Miss Kitty. She stood up, folding the material under her arm. "Come on, Emmie."

"Where are we going now, Miss Kitty?" I asked.

"I'm going to make this crepe into a shroud, I think," said Miss Kitty. She smiled.

CHAPTER *Twenty-Eight*

Summer grew like some animal. In the later days of July, it swallowed all the air with its increasing size. The bees grew, too, swelling until they became storehouses of sound; suspended on the butter-thick sky, their sound rose from out of them, and flattened. It spread in endless waves to meet with our ears.

I lay on the porch swing, with my nose fastened in one of the slats. The swing slid through space.

Light grew from the light bulb of sun. The air smelled of it. A gray sky streaked with butter yellow, salted with bees, their drone spreading out from them over the level plane of their existence; the stifled smell of bottled-up honeysuckle; the perpetual, slow, popping grease sound of Lucinda cooking hamburger. All sound was dulled. A headache wedged itself in between my eyebrows.

The world was rich—almost rotten with the lush smell of pine. My body, like a damp caramel candy, melted into the constant cool of it.

In this season, when eyeballs grew seared, when all became wrapped in yellow sun-dust, Verbena fastened her sights on Uncle's bathroom bush.

Perhaps it was because the bush was albino. In any case, it maintained a special place in the sensibilities of Verbena Fosbrink. She was determined, doggedly determined, to save it as

a symbol of her crusade—as a rallying cry to all the other as-
sorted flora of the world.

Uncle lived in constant fear that the bush would fall to Verbena's zealous trowel. His ears grew attuned to the sound of
her hesitant, shuffling step, to the secretive scraping at the
base of the window. He would spring off the john and zip up
his pants, all the time shouting, "Emmeline! Emmeline! It's
Verbena!"

At his cry I would rapidly extricate my nose from the slat of
the swing, and with one flying hand grab the handle of Glorio's birdcage. Howling, screaming, waving the cage wildly in
a dire manner, I would tear around the house, a slight and
bony apparition not unlike the wailing banshee.

It was with no little reason that Verbena was terrified of me.
First of all, I held the cage. She was petrified by the cage.
That was understandable.

I was petrified by the cage. Had it not been for tremendous
conditioning, I would never have had the courage to touch its
dingy brass at all.

Secondly—when I look back on it—there was me, like some
small and diving bird, mad with screams.

She would start up quickly with her blind eyes hidden behind the two panes of smoked glass. With her sunglasses, in
her whitened state, swathed from head to heel of foot in
clothing, she appeared to be a ghost as well, as if her filmy
substance were captured within the bounds of earthly vest-
ments. It was with a ghost's expression that she looked at me
—a look of incredulity that slipped fast into one of stark horror.

Slowly, almost carefully, she lowered her trowel and stared
at me. Then, as the impact hit her with full force, she would
desperately seize up the trowel and, scrambling from the earth
like some balloon hesitantly disengaged, leap to disappear
into the bushes that separated our house from Mrs. Larbuck's.

I always let her go.

Encumbered by so much clothing, her running was of necessity not the speediest. But I always let her go. I never knew what I'd do if I caught her.

By the time I had dispatched Verbena scuffling through Mrs. Larbuck's flora, all the ladies and Uncle Lamb would be leaning far over the porch railing trying to see the outcome of the struggle.

I can remember once turning back. My eyes lit upon my uncle. As he stood, leaning over the rail, with lines of anxiety carved too deeply into the flesh of his face, and his huge belly straining to meet with air through the manifold holes in his T-shirt, it seemed suddenly that I could see traces of me in him. It was a line of worry which brought one of our eyebrows up, and implanted over the other a small, pencil-thin, horizontal line. It was . . . suddenly the color of his eyes, so much like mine, and the arched bridge of his nose. . . . I had seen them in the mirror, and now, standing outside, I saw them in his face. It was almost startling, and I wondered, for that instant, if anyone else had ever noticed. His eyes met with mine. Almost as if he were ashamed, he lowered them. He shuffled toward the door. He was followed by the vapid and multicolored body of Mrs. Turncew.

The summer was punctuated with these moments. Locked within our bodies, our brains were baked out of us with the burn of the sun. The hills blistered and the acrid smell of them was blown through the country on a wind that was only a whisper in this oppressive heat of July.

Always . . . always etched on my memory: the stealthy animal shuffling of Verbena's clumsy feet, the dry upturning of yellow soil, and the cry of my uncle far away within my ears: "Emmeline! Emmeline! Emmeline!" The split second of pain as I drew my nose from the slat, the increasing difficulty in getting it out. The shock of air, and the fast moving, the whirl of world when all suddenly stopped—and I would be standing out in the back yard, the birdcage in my hand. It would be swinging, violently swinging. Then gentling, then slowing, then ceasing. The wet and sucking sound as the ladies once more lowered their large and damp mounds of flesh back into their chairs.

CHAPTER *Twenty-Nine*

Miss Kitty got her shroud back from the seamstress's the very same day that Mrs. Logg had the Boxwright brothers move her coffin into the parlor.

She laid it away for a few days. Then she took to taking it out and looking at it. Soon the time between each viewing shortened. Soon Miss Kitty began to try it on.

"Emmeline! Emmeline!" she would call. "Emmeline, get out of that swing and come help me on with this shroud. Girl! You hear!" She would drop things onto the roof—old perfume bottles, candy boxes—until I ran upstairs.

"Now, help me with this thing!" She would thrust her old arms into the air and shut her eyes tight closed. I would clamber up on her bed and slowly lower it over her stooped figure. She walked around in it, out of necessity taking very short steps from one end of the diminutive room to the other. She would turn around. "How do I look?"

Then one day she threw the slop jar out the window. When I came up, she was sitting on her bed cutting holes in the shroud—five of them: two for the arms, two for the feet, one for her skinny neck.

I sat down beside her. Upon questioning her, I found that Miss Kitty, being very practical and not counting eternity as long enough to get the full wear out of a good length of cloth, intended to use the shroud as a nightgown.

With my more steady hand on the scissors, we finished cutting the holes in the shroud, and tried it on her.

Miss Kitty cut a stunning picture in the shroud.

She stalked up and down the room, and then down and up the room. While outside in the world the crickets all began to chime and the shadows to deepen.

CHAPTER *Thirty*

Uncle no longer dared to step out of the bathroom.

Mrs. Turncew grew ever more militant in her guard. No longer content with a siege, she began making timid—but always bolder—attacks on the door. I could see the waiting in her face, the watchfulness, as I passed her in the hall. She sat always in her chair. Each day it seemed to loom higher, to become bloodier red in its plush velvet upholstery. I could see the threat hiding in her eyes.

She had placed an ottoman at her feet, a piece of furniture that took up some fourth of the width of the hall. His door, each time he tried to open it, clanked hard on the unyielding leather of it.

And in late July she got the key.

Uncle had, early in his confinement, procured a lock for which he also procured a key. The doors of the downstairs were thick and paneled, unlike the plywood slabs that so feebly shielded the upstairs doors. Once locked, the door was like the iron gate to some castle.

Uncle kept the key around his wide and fleshy neck on a shoestring gleaned from one of my ancient tennis shoes.

One day, as evening was just beginning to absorb the heat of day prior to spitting it back out at us, I heard, far off in the distant hollows of my ear, the distinct and stealthy sound of padded feet breaking against the soil. In exactly the same instant I heard Uncle's piercing cry, "Emmeline! Emmeline!"

With a sharp burst of pain, I twisted my nose out of the slat and, throwing my head around, caught first sight of Glorio's cage and then the cage itself. Swinging it wildly, I dived off the porch and galloped into the back yard, shrieking.

Verbena crouched by the bush. There was her brief look up; the horror catching in her face and then exploding over her entire body; her startled leap. Stopping, the world blowing round me, sounds, heart, feet, bushes breaking open as she dove through them . . . footsteps, swinging, stopping, almost stopping, stopping, stopping, fully stopping. Silence. Heart. And twilight, twilight suddenly all around me, and cool.

I looked around, steadying my feet in my shoes, and saw Uncle straining to see over the porch rail. I couldn't see his face, for it was growing too dark, but I could see his T-shirt. It shone white, and hanging down across it was the silver flash of the key.

I held the cage out far from me. From inside it I heard Glorio munching on his scabby flesh. Out of the stillness I heard voices.

"Lamb." It was Mrs. Turncew. "Lamb, don't go back inside. Not now. Have some lemon-limeade. I baked you a cake, with dates and raisins. It's cool and dark. Come and have some lemon-limeade with me and the ladies."

In the hastening night, her voice was soft with a sharp edge. It slit the air like a sword slitting gelatin. She was clinging onto his arm. I could see her waxy hand, her fingers around the flesh of it.

"Yes, yes," cooed the ladies. "Come out. The night is so cool."

I stepped towards the house.

The honeysuckle nodded in the brief wind that night's coming had caused.

Uncle turned toward the door.

"Lamb," said Mrs. Turncew. "Don't go back!"

Uncle Lamb looked at her. His voice shook. "Let me go,"

he said. With his own hand he started to unpry her fingers. With a sudden strength, Mrs. Turncew reached out and grabbed hold of the key around his neck. Uncle backed up quickly and twisted his neck around to go. It had been an unpremeditated gesture, but now Mrs. Turncew's mind had realized its possibilities. She held the key, held it with all her might, and thrashing against Uncle's bulky, panicked movement, she kept her fingers locked on his arm. Uncle twisted and slammed himself against the wall, and then, crying out and bolting for it, reached the front door. She clung, her dress sticking around her legs; from her throat came harsh, high animal cries.

I started to sudden life and ran up the porch steps. In the dim hall, I could see them struggling—flashes of white and light gray in the almost pitch dark of the narrow foyer. Uncle fell into the ottoman and twisted around. Except for the doglike yelps of Uncle and the shrill exclamations springing from Mrs. Turncew, there was no sound save that of their bodies breaking against furniture, save the mad scuffling of their feet.

Uncle's face twisted toward me, contorted with the strain on his neck, deep red, swollen with blood. His face was crazy; I realized it, and an unknown fear grabbed at my heart. My eyes went dim to everything around me, and I leaped forward—and it broke. The shoestring broke.

Uncle staggered back against the bathroom door. He lay against it, and for one instant his eyes met and held with Mrs. Turncew's; she looked slowly up from the key and bit of string she held in her hand. Then he darted into the bathroom.

Mrs. Turncew stood. Light, the last of it spun out of the sun, played falteringly on her, lighting up first one plane of her molten face, then another. She breathed, and in the stillness it was rasping; it swallowed every other sound. She lowered herself into her chair, still watching the key. Then she placed it in the hollow of her lap. She sat and watched the door.

CHAPTER *Thirty-One*

It was August.

Miss Rama sat on the front porch and delicately opened her legs and pulled the wet nylons off of them. Then she opened and closed her knees rapidly in an effort to get air into her body. Her knees struck against each other in the yellow dust of the morning; they made almost a ringing sound in the atmosphere spit out by a spiteful sun.

"This weather," Miss Rama observed, batting her old eyes and looking under the porch eaves at the scorched sky, "is the Devil's doings." As if struck suddenly by the resemblance, she directed herself at me. "Emmeline, how you can keep your nose stuck in that porch swing all day long is beyond me! It could make it grow a funny way—you know that?"

Miss Tibbitt, for some unaccountable reason—perhaps cause it was that particular day, rather than the day before or the day after—was nervous. She sat on the very edge of her chair, as if she were a marionette whose master had looped the strings around his wrist many times. Her strings were taut almost to breaking, and all portions of her body strained to listen to the sounds that floated on the sodden air of summer.

"Wait until you're older," observed Mrs. Logg happily. "You get those splotchedy things all over your face—bumps. Well sir, one day you're going to get a bump sitting there in that swing, and it will hold you in that slat tighter than if you were glued there with Epoxy. Have to take the porch swing apart around you." She scratched her thigh. "Either that or you die."

"This floor is dirty," said Miss Rama peevishly. She bent down and ran her finger over the floorboards and eyed the dust.

"Where's Kitty?" asked Mrs. Logg.

"She's upstairs in her shroud," I said.

As the month of July had aged and then turned, Miss Kitty had grown more and more vague. She was ninety-two that year. Slowly her eyes waxed over. Her voice lightened until the slightest feather of a breeze could carry it away.

Finally she had stopped dressing in day clothes altogether. She took to wearing her shroud all the time, only taking it off on those occasions when her daughter, Miss Runa, came down from up Wabash way and peeled it off in order to render it pure from its collection of chocolate stains, orange-juice stains, and the large, crusted globs of gruel that had spilt there and petrified. Miss Kitty lived in dread of these visits.

"Why can't that man clean this floor?" Miss Rama held her finger up. She gasped and pointed to a corner. "And there goes a silverfish!"

"Don't be silly, Rama, the only silverfish in this house are in the kitchen and my commode. Where's Nellcine Turncew?"

"In the kitchen with the silverfish," I muttered. "She's making greenies again."

"Well," said Mrs. Logg petulantly, "I just wish she'd get to work on those African violets in my coffin!"

"But Nellcine told you," said Miss Tibbitt, starting up a little, "there just isn't the right exposure where your coffin is, Mary. You'll simply have to content yourself with geraniums!"

Mrs. Logg looked stony.

Miss Tibbitt sighed and thrust a half of a browned carrot into Glorio's cage. It flew out.

I put a rummie into my mouth.

From the bathroom I could hear Uncle as he hummed old Indiana songs—songs about summer and Indiana, and the canal. I thought of a journey we had taken once, summers before, when I had been five, to Delphi, the town of the upstate Wabash and Erie.

We drove along cornfields quiet with memories of the past, dry with the heat of summer's sun. Delphi is small now, and faded. It's like a sweet, perfect rose crushed many years since between the pages of a picture album, and it sits in silence. A stillness about it which is it—as if the town is only a shadow's thought, and not there at all. It breathes not at all, only silent, only still, only shy. A slow, soft hush. Be quiet, it says. We are knowing ourselves. We are—remembering ourselves. And the quiet flutters from tree to tree like a butterfly, and soft, yellow-flashing with limpid light, it is a reflection of leaves on the river wall.

> Way down upon the Wabash,
> Such land I've never known . . .
> If Adam had passed over it,
> This soil he'd surely own,
> He'd say it was the garden
> He played in, when a boy . . .
> And straight pronounce it Eden . . .

Uncle had led me beneath a bridge to see the Wabash and Erie. It was a narrow ditch, perhaps a car's length across, sunken, innocent of any siding such as I had imagined it—innocent of locks, of footpaths, cat rails, hand rails . . . The turf was its wall. It was covered with a thick coating of green slime. In the places split by cracks in its vegetable covering, I could see the brownness of a leaf-filled, weed-choked water. I saw the Wabash and Erie, fast fading into earth, when I was five, and I saw the ancient trees that were Delphi waiting for eternity. And when I was five, I understood my uncle.

Uncle now slept in the bathroom. He had begun to when Mrs. Turncew sold her house and took old Mrs. Winslow's corner room. One night he had simply not come out. From that time on, he never came out except upon those occasions when Verbena stalked, and her hesitant foot was heard scraping in our grass.

I lay on the porch swing and listened to his voice as it stopped and then started again, assuming vocalization only in parts, singing with half of his mind. "Rue"; "The Wabash Cannonball"; "In the pines, in the pines, where the sun never shines, going to whistle when the cold wind blows . . ."; and "The E-Rye-Ee was a-rising, the gin was gettin' low. I won't get a drink, I really don't think, till I get to Buffalo—I—Oh, then I get to Buffalo!"

I left his meals outside his door. Sometimes, when none of the ladies were around and Mrs. Turncew had decamped for a moment, I would get him a can of beer and a cold glass— Falstaff beer, with the picture of the state on it, in memory of the summers he had spent on the chicken coop, roundly cursing the sun that robbed Indiana's hills of sweetness. I would put it in the laundry chute that served both the bathroom and my room, unbeknownst to Mrs. Turncew. Drinking it in the cool greenness of the bathroom, perhaps he envisioned the hills gone to brown, like decayed sugar, like the burnt hair of a land laid bare and smelling of acid on the rare tufts of heated wind. I always imagined he did.

I floated momentarily in the silence that swallowed the porch. Then, "Emmeline!"

I sprang up and grabbed the cage. My nose was shot with an agony of pain.

"Emmeline!" Uncle called—but it was not a Verbena cry. I

lowered the cage. The cry was softer; it was slower, more hesitant.

"Yes," I said. I pulled my shirt down.

The ladies peered at me. Miss Rama lowered her spectacles on her nose and glared.

"Could you come in here?"

I lifted up the cage cover and looked at Glorio. He chewed his leg in the darkness. Offended, he spit out his leg and glowered at me. I set the cage down. I walked through the door and into the darkness of the hall.

The chair was empty. It rose always as a reminder of Mrs. Turncew. Her presence was there yet. I had to slide past the ottoman to get at the door. Before it, I paused—it seemed a long time since I had seen Uncle. Finally I turned the knob and opened it.

The room was dark—bottle-green now, for the bush had grown even larger. It spread with its thousands of narrow arms, embracing the whole of the window.

Beside Uncle, on the floor by the commode, was the copy of *Shakespeare's Works* that he had always kept by his bed. He had told me once that he had wanted to be an actor in his youth. He had joined a road company that traveled from Midwestern town to Midwestern town, stopping three nights and presenting three religious stories—the story of Ruth, of Gideon, of Esther. In Terre Haute the terebinth tree fell on him during a performance of *The Story of Gideon* and broke his leg in three places. The road manager told him he ought to stay out of those places, and fired him. It was Uncle's only break.

His sole source of light was the window, which gave only slivers of sun now. They were thrown on the floor in a haphazard fashion, as if out of a shavings bag, and they shifted with the slow and sultry moving of the bush's tiny waxen leaves, the opium nod of the off-white, death-ragged blossoms, in what an outsider might term a "breeze." Chaucy people knew that it was merely the long, slick, slippery, gray rubber octopus of summer, shifting positions as he slept upon the town.

Uncle sat on the commode with his belly overlapping to meet with belly—he had once been an active man—and that belly reaching out to touch with a further extension of this great and magnificent part of him.

The diabolical halo circled his head, but was only noticeable when, with a sudden change of the light slivers, it became bathed in the yellow dust of sun.

Sheathed in such darkness, the room was unfamiliar to me. It was as if I had not seen it before. But it seemed as if it should have been dark from the very beginning, for darkness suited it. In the dark, the cool, the near twilight, it was a world apart, a ghost existence, a half and haunted world.

Uncle looked up from his hands and gestured to me.

I blinked hard, trying to accustom my eyes to the light.

Beside me was the water heater, an ominous creation composed of some metal corresponding to brass in every way but price. It sizzled. It hissed. From its valves it occasionally sent water, invariably cold. The water heater was paranoid as well as antagonistic. If you in any way violated its valves, it would rear back like a nervous colt and commence to rattle and groan and make savage overtures in a manner most alarming. This apparatus sat eyeing Uncle each day of the summer. Now, upon my entering, it switched its focus point and proceeded to favor me with all kinds of hostile grimaces.

" 'Lo, Emmie," said Uncle.

I walked toward him, suddenly shy.

"Thank you for the . . ." With a wave of his hand he indicated the modest but growing stack of beer cans by the laundry chute opening.

I nodded. I held out a rummie.

He shook his head. "Sit down," he offered. He gestured at a

red-and-white stool that observed, in large letters, that brushing one's teeth after each meal was the first step on the road to greater hygiene. It was my stool, given to me by my dentist, a former football player named Dr. Boker. Dr. Boker came in with a novocain needle as if he was throwing a long pass. I was terrified of him. I viewed the stool with apprehension. I sat down gingerly.

"Emmeline," he said, rubbing his forehead. "How . . . old are you?"

"Eight," I said, "years and seven months. Would you like some . . ." I held out my bag of rummies. Uncle eyed it and rubbed his forehead again. Even in the dimness, though the shadows played on his face, I could discern the sweat lying in the creases and wrinkles that composed it.

The sound of the women as they sat on the front porch, the buzz of their sporadic conversation, came to us from the porch; as yeast rises, it rose and, fermenting with empty air bubbles, evaporated into the solemn, ever-watchful sky. For this brief moment, the bees and the ladies exchanged places in their sounds. The buzz of the bees died; from the countless black, hairy monsters that hovered on the thick air came only the wistful flutter of tiny-veined, membraned wings.

From the kitchen rose the smell of greenies.

I looked around Uncle's hideaway, at Uncle; in this light he seemed a suggestion of a world in another dimension. I sat looking at him for a minute, perhaps. It seemed like more. In that one tiny minute in that small room it seemed as if this bubble of green and the man it sheltered were too fragile, that they were things too dream-born to endure.

Uncle sat on the commode, his face a pattern of leaves. The *Shakespeare,* in his hands now, seemed an appendage of him. I had a sudden flash of vision: I saw spears of sunlight falling hard across Uncle's face—spears of light once kept out and away by the branches of the bush, not native to this greener world. And I realized that, big though it was, the bush was but a foot or two wide; its roots were not yet firm in soil.

The stuffed terrier fell out of the linen closet.

" 'Now is the winter of our discontent made glorious summer by this sun of York!' " said Uncle, weakly. " 'Glorious summer . . . ,' my foot!"

I stood up quickly and thrust the stuffed terrier back into the closet.

It toppled out.

"What's that woman doing in there?" His voice was hushed. "She's not in the foyer, is she?"

I shook my head.

He breathed out and leaned back.

"She's baking greenies," I said.

An eye fell out of the terrier and rolled across the bathroom floor. I got on my hands and knees, and went prowling in search of it.

"Greenies!" he exclaimed, remembering no doubt the incident with the stomach pump. He covered his face in his hands. He removed them a few seconds later to reveal a strained and haunted visage. I looked up at him from my all-fours position. I didn't want to—it was impossible not to. We remained, suspended for some moments. A shudder of emotion such as I had never seen before distorted his face. For a second we were no longer what we had always been. No longer casual allies, no longer held by that single strand of invisible camaraderie, sitting together on a swing, blocking out Mrs. Turncew's body with our own. He was examining me to find himself in me. In that second he probed into every line, every feature of my face, and pulled away my skin to look at the pulsating thing that was my brain—to look and find if it were his.

"I'm looking for the eye," I said at last. "It fell out."

Uncle sat up.

I found the eye behind the wastepaper basket and popped it

into my blue-jeans pocket. There was no use trying to wedge it back into the stuffed terrier's eye socket.

"We were speaking of your age," Uncle said.

The heavy thing that had caught on my heart a moment before relaxed a bit, then slowly, like the forced fragmentation of a mosaic, I dissolved it and put it away from me. "I'm eight," I repeated helpfully. I stuck a rummie in between my teeth.

"Eight," said Uncle, not entirely looking at me. "Ah—eight, you say?" He rubbed his forhead. With his finger he dug deep into the sweat that lay in its cracks. "Sit down, Emmie."

I sat down once more on the little red-and-white greater-hygiene stool and peered up at him.

Uncle looked down on me. "Emmeline . . ." He looked at me. "Dammit," he said. "I can't . . . Come up here." He patted his lap.

I stood up and clambered on. I looked expectantly at him.

"Emmeline," he said. "You remember me telling you about your mother . . . and your father, don't you? About her deciding that you were a figment of her imagination . . . are you following me?"

I nodded.

"You were very little then."

I nodded.

Uncle looked very sad. "And I didn't think . . ." He looked at me. "You were so little. No one else remembers how little you were, except Miss Kitty. You had tiny hands, and fingernails like little pearls, and even when you were born, you had hair like hers. . . ." He touched my hair momentarily; in the green light it fell from my pigtails a red, heavy bronze. "I thought it might be easier, while you were young, if you thought . . . I met her when she was still a little girl, only fifteen . . . I thought . . ."

"Yes?" I said.

"Yes," he said. He stopped.

"Want a rummie?" I held out a rummie.

Uncle shook his head violently. He wiped his forehead. I smiled at him. He bit his lip.

"Emmeline," he said. "I'll wait, I think . . . I'll tell you . . . some other time, OK?" He slid me off his lap. "Go on," he said.

I stood up and pulled up my blue jeans, puzzled. I walked to the door.

"Emmeline," Uncle called.

I turned around.

"Emmeline," and his voice was soft and pleading, "don't become a woman."

I looked at him, trying to see behind his eyes. The light cast down from the bush swam in circles on his darkened face. And I promised him. I said, "I won't."

CHAPTER Thirty-Two

The second week in August, Miss Kitty's daughter Runa visited her, and once more peeled the shroud off her old body to wash it. Miss Kitty refused to put anything else on while it was in the wringer washer. She sat up on her narrow bed with her long, bony arms wrapped around herself, and her feet dangling over the edge of the bed. Sitting in a draft, she caught a summer's chill—it was the bullet that killed her.

She was sick all that week. I was drawn up to her room out of a sort of morbid fascination. I would sneak quietly in, holding my bag of rummies close to my chest.

She did not know me. She called me by my name, but she thought I was my mother on some occasions, her daughter Runa on others.

"Emmeline," she would say to me. Above, the curtains moved with the barely circulating air of early August. The sun cast its eyes across her faded coverlet. "You're carrying a child. Mend your ways and stop flirting out on Mr. Lamb. Don't lie your face off at me, girl. You think I don't have eyes?"

"No ma'am," I said. "These here are rummies—in a bag."

I was forbidden to give her any. In the past we had sat, the two of us, and eaten them. She had gummed them, drooling molasses down her chin until it had hardened to amber beads on her white, parchment skin.

"I wish I could give you some, Miss Kitty. Miss Runa says I'm not to. You can't have sugar or such."

Miss Kitty rolled her head feebly on the pillow. "Leave Sumie Delaine's brother alone," she said. "You've got a good husband. You've got a little girl. Why do you want Laurey Delaine for?"

I was puzzled. I couldn't figure out who she was talking about—me, or my mother, or Miss Emmeline Russell. I shifted from foot to foot.

The week slowly passed; Miss Kitty got worse and worse, and she talked nonsense, reaching into the past and drawing up old conversations and old people. She told me the days of her first husband, and I became her husband, her daughters, her sons, her mother. Once I was old Mr. Fitz-Simons's cow. Often I was Runa, and the puzzling combination of my mother and Miss Emmeline that her ancient imagination had conjured up.

Friday came, and in the night she died.

An hour or two before, I had sat up on the corner of her bed and listened to her for the last time. She rocked her head back and forth on the pillow. Each breath she took was a whistle. I sat and watched her old face as it caught the light, watched the brief and butterfly shadows waver across it.

"Emmeline," she whispered.

"Yes, Miss Kitty," I said.

"When that child of mine gets here . . . when Runa gets here, you tell her that I mean to be buried in my shroud. You tell her that."

"Yes, Miss Kitty."

"Runa? Did you hear that?"

I looked around the room for Runa, but I knew Miss Kitty was addressing me. Her eyes on my face were milky.

"Yes, ma'am," I said.

"You were always my best daughter, Runa. Runa! Where's Louise and Trixie? Where are those girls!? Emmeline, you make sure that Runa does that. Name it Kitty, pretty please, for Kitty?" Her voice fell away, and she turned to look at the bureau.

I knelt over her. "Miss Kitty!" I whispered. "Miss Kitty!"

Suddenly with strength she turned her head over on the pillow and looked at me with her eye suddenly gone clear. "Your uncle had no sister," she said levelly. "Emmeline Russell was your mother."

CHAPTER *Thirty-Three*

I watched them gather her body up and take it to Boxwright Brothers'. They kept her there. She never came back to the house.

I told Miss Runa about the shroud. Miss Runa was plump and pink; her hair was pink, too. Even in black she looked all pink. Her eyeglasses had pink butterflies roosting on their faintly lavender tips. She took me on her plump knee and smiled at me, and told Mrs. Logg that she hated to say it, but she was really glad—and wasn't Mrs. Logg?—that Mother had gone to her reward at last, for the Lord sometimes allowed people to live too long, didn't he? No criticism of the Lord intended, of course, but I was not to worry about it; Miss Runa would take care of it all just like Mother would have wanted it, and if I felt like it, why didn't I run upstairs right now and get the picture of Joseph Cotten that Mother had kept on the bureau, she was sure that Mother would have wanted Emmeline to have it.

At the funeral the casket was open. Miss Kitty was wearing a black suit and stockings, and a little stretch of lace over her sparse hair.

I looked at her, and then I looked at Miss Runa, who was interesting herself with the Apostles' Creed and a corsage of black orchids—her husband was a florist—that kept pulling the lapel of her black suit down with its weight—an action resulting in an ungraceful line.

Mrs. Logg hit me in the side with her elbow and pointed in her hymnal to a stretch of print that I had never before seen. "This is what we always read at funerals," she said. "Pull up your drawers."

Dimly I wondered where the shroud was. I wondered why it wasn't on Miss Kitty. I had told Miss Runa. I had told her as plain as day just after Miss Kitty had died, just like Miss Kitty had told me to.

The church collapsed to their knees in unison, Mrs. Logg dragging me down with her. My nose was forced down into the wooden backs of the pews. I couldn't think. It had been but a day since Miss Kitty had died, leaving me with those strange words, and in the numbness that was the wake of her death I hadn't had time to . . . sit down and think about it. The ladies had run back and forth, up and down the stairs. Miss Tibbitt, in a fit of bereavement, had tried to make Boxwright Brothers' use Mrs. Turncew's coffin for Miss Kitty. She had thrown herself on it and dug out the African violets with her hands, while Mrs. Turncew, also on her knees, had desperately tried to put them right back in again. There was a great smell of lilies and orchids in the house—the white, waxy flowers, the rubbery, too-green stems everywhere; their scent choked the air. And I couldn't figure out where the shroud was. Miss Kitty's shroud!

". . . dust to dust . . ."

Where was it? Hadn't Miss Runa been able to find it? Had the Boxwright brothers done something with it? Had the doctors at the Alice Babcock Chaucy Hospital? Had the nurse? Had the minister?

Reverend Mr. Brick spoke the name of her husband. I started up with surprise. He had been dead forty years. Miss Kitty, even when she had thought I was he, had forgotten his name. Morton Pollard. Mrs. Morton Pollard. They were burying Mrs. Morton Pollard; she'd been dead for . . .

Had Runa forgotten?

They were burying the wrong woman! They were not burying . . . a thousand thoughts struck my mind at once. The
woman who had died was not Miss Kitty, and Miss Kitty
would have been the only one to know if it was true what he
said, the woman who died, Mrs. Morton Pollard. Miss Kitty
would know. Miss Kitty would . . . I could go home and
find her, and that would prove that they were burying the
wrong . . .

I started to rise, to stop it, stop it until they could find the
shroud and the real Miss Kitty in it. Mrs. Logg pulled me violently down onto my knees. "You are in the presence of God!
Grace, child! What were you doing?!"

And my chance was gone. It was gone. The coffin lid was
swung shut and latched, and six old men—the round and
florid sons and grandsons of Mrs. Morton Pollard—swung in
line, with difficulty pried the coffin off the bier, and staggered
down the aisle.

I watched them do it with the panic that was still in me, and
leaping up again, I started after them. Mrs. Logg fastened her
heavy, meaty hand on my shoulder. "Stop that this instant!"
she commanded. "I'm ashamed of you, carrying on like a five-
year-old! Now stand stock still! One move more out of you,
and you'll see who's not going to get to go to the cemetery!"

With her hand clapped on my shoulder bone, we walked
out into the sunshine outside the church.

"Well," murmured Miss Tibbitt, sniveling into her handker-
chief.

Runa adjusted her corsage once more.

"You have one thing to be thankful for," Miss Tibbitt said.
"At New Hope Cemetery, they always have morning services.
At sunrise. Isn't that sweet?"

I jerked away from Mrs. Logg's grasp and rushed down the
street. Behind me I heard the sound of her calling after,
threats alternating with pleas. I shook my head back and forth
to drown her out. I ran two blocks and then walked two. I

wasn't crying. I picked up a mock orange and threw it down. It splintered into a hundred pieces.

The street was cool, shaded with trees. The shiftings of their leaves formed patterns of shadow and cool. Everything was silent and still and green.

I walked until I got to the house, and then, turning, I stepped onto the walk. I shut the door softly behind me. I knew he was in the bathroom, that even now he heard my footsteps on the floor, that he was trying, trying to distinguish them from Mrs. Turncew's. I could have called out. But I went upstairs. I took off my socks and laid them in my patent-leather shoes. I lay down on my bed. The sunlight played across my body in fingers of heat.

CHAPTER *Thirty-Four*

During the reception, Miss Runa came upstairs to me and brought a brownie and a glass of fruit punch. She put her hands on my head, her dry, warm palms resting a moment on my ears, and then went downstairs. I put the food on my window sill and slowly changed out of my sweat-soaked, starched dress, and into a pair of soft and faded cotton shorts and a white, limp blouse that fell cool against my chest. Then I ate the brownie and poured the fruit punch out the window onto the porch roof. It gathered momentarily in the gutter, then dribbled out of sight.

I tiptoed to the end of the hall, and slipping open the stained-glass window, the cup and plate in my hand, I wedged myself through it. Sitting on the kitchen roof, I slid down the shingles on my fanny. When I reached the gutter, I closed my eyes and jumped to the ground. I took the paper plate and cup and made my way down to the garbage pails. From inside, I could hear the chatter of nearly eighty reception guests. The hot, doughy smell of overly rich food rolled from the house. I opened the lid to put my plate and cup in. The shroud was there.

I stood staring at it a second. Then I looked at the window, squinting in the light. I had not thought for so long—even finding this confused me. She had to be dead. Miss Kitty would not have let them throw it away if she were alive. Miss Kitty had died.

Then, in the gathering afternoon, I put down my paper

plate and cup and picked the shroud up. I folded it and put it under my arm. I shinnied up the post and back up to the stained-glass window. I laid it in my drawer and placed the picture of Joseph Cotten over it.

CHAPTER *Thirty-Five*

The next day I opened the door to the front proch and felt a shaft of yellow fall across me. On the floorboards of the porch, I made out the shadow of Mrs. Logg, her foot on the rocker, rocking her jetty of bosom.

I pulled up my pants and walked out onto the porch, down the steps.

"Where are you going?" asked the formidable bust. As if she knew where in truth my heart and feet were bound, she shook her finger at me and warned ominously, "Step on a crack and you break your mother's back." I turned around suddenly and looked at her. With a hairy eyebrow, she indicated the line that had been freshly redrawn after Mr. Rose-nblum's latest attack on it with the watering hose.

I slowly took my eyes off her—wondering if she knew, if the other ladies, with their blank, discontented faces, knew—and walked down the steps, out onto the road to Beekerman's Hill.

Beekerman's Hill was composed of two sides—as hills are wont to be—one side housing that portion of the populace of Chaucy who had already met their God, the other sporting a chain of some thirty-two sewer pumps that squatted in single file to meet with the crest of the next hill. This, not being distinguished by a cemetery, did not have a name.

Beekerman's Hill—the sewer side—was my favorite place. I stood at the foot of it and held my two hands up before my eyes, lowering them just enough so that I could not see below my height—yet they were there, a whole line of them, melting into the sunset. Sewer pipes are omnipresent.

I walked over and sat down on the nearest one. I looked at the sun, which, since its afternoon fury, had notably softened —it lay plump, and ripe as an egg yolk, sliding within its fragile membrane, floating just above the horizon.

Far in the distance, caught against the setting of the summer's sun, the pumps stood black, like distant sentinels.

The shadows of the trees through which the line had been cut fell sharp and black across the grass, which stretched to meet with the shadows of the trees on the further side.

Somewhere, from far away, a bird's cry rose hysterical and high, then stopped; it was as if the day had taken the bird by its warm and trembling throat, and ceased it of life.

I knelt and picked some flowers; they were wild iris. Smaller than hothouse iris, without the velvet and lush color of their pampered relations, they were light and lavender, tiny and fragile. Their pistils were as slender as the feelers of a butterfly. They seemed to me more lovely—like faeries caught in soil and growing against their will—than any other flower in the world. They grew wild about the base of the sewer pipe, and stretched in lines, sometimes in fields, deep into the dark stillness of the woods.

I held them before my nose and looked through their membrane petals at this world. I closed my eyes very hard and said, "Remember this. Remember the way it looked, and the way it smelled. Remember as long as you live. Remember him . . ." I stopped. I let go of the flowers and pulled my pants up.

Inside my body I felt stirrings—it was as if a cold and sharp steel rod had sprung up in me and pierced my skull. I looked down at my narrow body, and I knew it would change. I looked at the world, with its brutal sun, and it would change, too. I turned and started for the road.

[*1* 7 9

I was walking back from the rummies man's store. The weather waited. The land was filled with a roar of silence, the steady, insistent roar of its waiting. Suddenly, from deep within the hills, the thin piping of a bird climbed on the air, as if the earth had been slit like a pie and the blackbirds freed. The sound pressed into my heart. Then silence, returning, filled my ears. From the sky, the sun stared out from its yellow aura. The leaves hovered on the trees.

I passed the statue of Miranda Milk, Homer's Indian bride. It stood five feet nine in bare feet—it was her authentic size, and her mighty frame supported one hundred and eighty pounds as it had in life. So encrusted with dirt was the statue of Miranda Milk that flies winging into her caught on her external layer, trapped, living a living death as new layers of river mud, mud of all sorts, and time laid still another coat of their dulled polish to her already-thick slime capsule.

In but a little while these flies became only darker spots of pigment in the varied color scheme of Miranda Milk, née Big Moose. New ones were added daily. The days, years—all had made their contributions. By the time I was eight years old, the statue resembled nothing so much as a pile of rotting fish eggs. The dirt of the ages had found its way to her formidable granite hide and taken residence there.

I walked up Nation Street.

I thought about the rummies man as I had last seen him— he had been stuffing the rummies into my pink and sticky sack. I remembered his voice as it swam from the darkness of his back room:

> "Immortal and divine, great Bacchus, god of wine,
> Create me by adoption your son
> In hopes that you'll comply
> That my glass will ne'er run dry,
> Nor my smiling little cruiskeen lawn, lawn, lawn,
> Nor my smiling little cruiskeen lawn."

He had looked at me, his face a maze of knotted muscle. "One extra," he said. "You're a steady customer." With his liver-spotted hands, he pulled another rummie from its bin, sticky with the heat of his hands and the day.

There was a very faded picture of a place with many big and rich-colored flowers on it behind his counter.

"See that," said the rummies man. "Puerto Rico." He said it softly, musically. "Pu-erto Rico. Si, si," he said. "Where the rummies come from." He turned and looked at me—oddly. Then, sticking his hand once more into the bin, he pulled out another rummie and silently handed it to me.

He slipped from the front room into his narrow workshop. I heard the clatter of bottles as he drew something from off the shelf.

The leaves brushed each other as they moved with the slight wind. It was a gentle wind, soft and slow, mellow. I picked up a leaf, holding it as I walked; its waxen back showed tremulous veins as I held it up to light. I traced them with my finger. Movement was all up, drawn high in the August sky.

I climbed the steep bluff—and higher—and my calves ached with the climbing, and grew hard and knotted. At the crest of the hill, I could see the factory as it loomed; at this distance, enveloped in sunlight, it seemed an almost spiritual place, casting its overlarge and abstract shadow in panels onto the blowsy grass that lay around it and caressed, with its blowing, the foundation.

Chaucy.

It was the town where I had been born. I looked over it.

It was swallowed in the belly of something ominous, something too slow for words, something that gave an extra second to each action and to this feeling in me, this eruption of numbness. The whole town was bathed in an unearthly light. I stood on the bluff that morning as the town lay in stupor, and I felt a tightening of my heart and a tightening of my thoughts. . . .

I took the leaf out of my pocket and let it fall. It drifted to the ground in an elaborate series of falls, lacy swoops, and then landed, its veins pressed into the ground.

Far off was the bridge, spanning the sullen Wabash. Once there had been a man who stayed by the River Road and attracted little girls with the pennies he let fall from his gray overcoat pocket. While they were kneeling to pick them up, he snatched them around their fannies and hotfooted it to a shack where he cut them into little pieces and then threw them into the river. On summer days, when our sun had migrated to Bermuda, leaving only a pale rendition of itself glimmering in a white Indiana sky, when tufts of clouds impaled themselves on the narrow strips of barely blue that laced the atmosphere, I used to stand on the catwalk of the Candlemar Section Bridge, looking for fingers.

I thrust my hands far into my pockets, cramming them down where the cotton stretched tight across my buttocks, and looked. Then I turned around and started up Jean Street.

The shudder of leaves in this, the conception point of the town, rose louder on my ears. I passed Mr. Rose-nblum's house. That worthy man leaned out the window and waved to me.

From the porch I could see Mrs. Logg as she squatted in state, Miss Rama as she scratched herself and flung her legs apart to the accompaniment of clattering bones. They assaulted me with cries.

"Emmeline! Emmeline Lamb, have you got your shoes on?"

"Don't you set your *foot* on that man's property!"

I knelt down in the dirt—it existed in great abundance on our front lawn—and picked up a clump of soil. It was dry; it smelled chemical. It melted in my fingers. I wiped my hands on my dress front and crouched froglike in the brittle grass.

Miss Rama slapped at the air with her church pamphlet. A bee lowered itself, taking off around her in slow, ever-descending circles, shaking all the time, not unlike Flash Gordon's spaceship coming in for a landing, until it came to rest on her shoulder. It gave her ear the eye.

Miss Rama sat up very still and straight.

"Miss Mary!" bellowed Mrs. Logg. "Everybody can see your bloomers when you sit like that! Do you want everybody to see your bloomers?"

"They're not my bloomers!" I shouted. "They're my shorts. I'm wearing them under my dress!"

"They're your bloomers if you're wearing them under that dress! Close your shanks!"

I closed my knees, an action which brought my posterior even nearer to Mother Earth.

The bee decided that Miss Rama's ear was none too tasty a morsel. It flew musingly away.

Miss Tibbitt flung Glorio out the window, holding him by his hind foot. She shook him vigorously. "He needs an airing!" she shouted.

Glorio, his triangular head swinging to and fro with alarming suppleness, gave me the eye.

I stood, and for that one minute I was suddenly afraid of the ladies, afraid of the porch, afraid of the house, afraid of him. What Miss Kitty had told me . . . In my mind I saw myself going to the laundry chute, looking far down into its black shaft, and seeing one of my mother Emmeline's diamonds; I saw myself turning around in the pantry and falling over her chest, with ER stamped on it; I saw the locket I had found springing open, and my picture there. Why hadn't he told me? Why . . . Why hadn't he had the courage to . . . I thought of my whole life spent in this town, not knowing, not knowing . . .

I walked slowly to the porch and up the steps. I saw Mrs.

[*183*

Turncew sitting in the shadows of the hall, her eyes intent on the door to the bathroom, and my heart was hard.

I lay down on the swing; my skin stuck to it fleetingly and then pulled free as I settled onto its water-saturated, salty-tasting boards. My lip was cut, cut by hard kernels of popcorn that I had eaten the day before. I pressed my salty finger to the wound, and inside I could feel the steady, small pounding of a tiny blood vessel, why, why, why? And my dulled mind— why? Tears hurried out, and then, slowly, painfully, I forced them back into my head.

Miss Tibbitt came out onto the front porch. "I put Glorio in the pantry," she said. "It's the coolest place in the house. Why, in the summertime, mind you, as much as I like God's good light . . ." She squinted. "I'd like for all the rooms to have no windows to them." She sat down in a chair and, picking up a palm fan, began a feeble attack on the air.

Orson leapt out of the bushes and descended with a sanguinary cry on an ivy leaf.

Mrs. Logg solemnly procured her knitting and, investing me with a series of malevolent glances—each one cut into me like a knife thrusting under my skin—started a slow, metallic clicking that grew until it swallowed all other sound but the sound of my brain pounding in my ears, the dull, straining pain sound pulling at my eyes. "Yes, the Lord's light is good," she said, directing her statements at me. "The Lord is merciful. He cares for all."

Blurrily I tried to think of Joshua's merry decimation of Ai. The throbbing in my body spread beyond me; it set even the air I lay in to beating. Samuel's fight with the Lord about the murder of Saul, I thought.

"Where are my number-nine knitting needles?" asked Mrs. Logg suspiciously.

"Rama had them last," said Miss Tibbitt.

"In by the wringer washer on the pots shelf," said Miss Rama, striking her knees together.

184]

Moses and the plagues on Egypt, Job, his sons, his daughters, his camels . . .

Mrs. Logg stood. She turned her bosom toward the door.

I heard it.

The low shuffle of Verbena in the tall grass. I tensed on the swing, fighting the yellow mire that reached for my eyes from the sun—it rolled like the tune of some unsung, unknown song. Then sharply, slitting it, his voice cut like a trapped bird. "Emmeline! Emmeline!"

I started to rise, but then the thought sank into me—he didn't love you, he didn't tell you, he didn't love you, he didn't tell you, he didn't love . . .

"Emmeline! Emmeline! It's Verbena!"

I heard the panicked scraping of her trowel in the parched earth.

I closed my eyes and closed up my face; he didn't love you, he didn't tell you, he didn't . . .

"Emmeline! *Emmeline!*" I forced the tears out. I pushed them out through my closed eyes. They jerked forward and cut with their sting along my nose, and I wouldn't listen, I wouldn't . . .

"Emmeline!" I . . . "EMMELINE!"

His voice was full of anguish, and it cut across me. Suddenly the tears burst forward. I pulled and twisted, trying to get free, but my nose wouldn't come out of the porch slat. I climbed to my knees and jerked. I swayed to the right, to the left . . .

"Emmeline!"

I stuck a finger up and poked it through the swing from the bottom. I fell into the moist, hot wood and wrenched my head, throwing it back, twisting it, pulling it . . .

There came a loud crash from the bathroom. Mrs. Turn-cew's voice streaked out, "Lamb! Lamb! I'm coming in! LAMB!"

"Get Glorio!" I screamed. "Get Glorio! *Get Glorio!*" The

tears were all over me. I couldn't see. I hammered my fists into the wood of the swing. "GET GLORIO!" I wrenched at my nose.

"I'm coming in, Lamb! I'm coming in!" I could hear scufflings around the door.

I screamed and screamed. I could hear the mad sound of Verbena's surprised digging, and the crashing sounds in the hall, and my own brain screaming and . . . I kicked the swing. I beat my hands against it.

Mrs. Logg came roaring out of the house. She held a scrap of canvas in her hand. "Alice Tibbitt! What have you got to say for yourself! That *rabbit* ate Emmeline's mother's portrait!"

"Lamb! Lamb! I'm coming in!"

"No! Stand out of my way, stand out . . ." He . . . there was a rattling of the key. . . .

The bush fell.

I could hear in the sudden stillness—like a breath, it hit the ground and then billowed up, its wooden throat cut from soil. I sunk into the porch swing and my tears came fast, swelling up inside of me—my eyes were not big enough to let them out. . . .

"Free!" howled Verbena. "Free!" An unearthly howl of triumph . . . "Free!"

My nose, without my moving, slid out. I lay there, crying into the wood.

Then came summer's cool. It came, and it swept the town with a sweetness gleaned from secret sources; the trees swelled with it and danced. The scent of honeysuckle and a thousand ragged roses blossomed on the air. A pale ice revolved and spun around the ladies.

Mrs. Turncew wandered onto the porch and, in silence, stood there.

From far away, like the cries of a distant cat caught high in a tree, I could hear the cries of my father.